Zombies vs Bikers

Zombies vs Bikers

By

Paul Ballinger

Other Books from Paul Ballinger:
Cellmates (2009)
Manto (2011)

ISBN: 978-1-105-27741-2
Published by Lulu.com
Printed and Distributed by Lulu.com
Cover by: Paul Ballinger & Jason Scott

Dedication:

To all those people who enjoy reading about the Weird, the Unusual, and sometimes the Just Plain Goofy. And of course, to the serious Zombie lovers of the world.

And to all the Bikers who know that every ride can bring you face-to-face with something new, weird, unusual, or just plain goofy. And of course, to all the biker lovers of the world.

And as always, to my Sidekick Kathy who's always there for me and loves me even when I'm weird, unusual, or just plain goofy.

And to Jason Scott, author of the Shift of the Dead series for his inspiration and technical help.

Hope ya'all have as much fun reading this strange adventure as I did writing it.

Approximately sixty miles south of Cincinnati is a town in northern Kentucky called Critterden. It's a town of some thirty thousand people most of which grew up in the area on their parents' farms then later moved to town where things were more convenient. Most of the locals, especially the youth, refer to the place as; "Critter Town."

Directly across the Kentucky River from Critterden is a small community of about forty families. Some still live on small farms, but there is a subdivision of nice homes that had been built back when the building craze was running rampant.

The homes had been built to be an "upscale" community where one could enjoy the beauty of nature and still be a couple of miles from the town of Critterden, and within a thirty-minute drive to larger cities in the northern Kentucky area. The building boom busted however, like the over-ripe cherry of a horny virgin, and rather than let the homes sit and rot away the builders dropped their prices about forty-five percent enabling some of the local families to purchase a home that was much nicer than the farm-house they'd grown up in.

This small community has no official name, though nearly all the locals refer to it as "Little

Critter." Little Critter has a small elementary school, small branch of the post office, a police sub-station, a small mom and pop grocery store, and two churches; one Baptist and one Catholic.

The two churches are always arguing back and forth, but it hasn't come to open gunfire yet. There too is the area's largest cemetery, which also serves the town of Critterden and which the Catholics wish was full of Baptists, and the Baptists would like to fill with Catholics if they could do it without incurring God's wrath.

Next to the cemetery is the large county jail, which houses an average of a hundred inmates, most of which are serving time for petty crimes. A few, however, are awaiting transfer to the state prison.

There are also three bars scattered throughout the community which are often warring with each other for customers, though it has developed into open gunfire only twice in recent history. The most popular of which was Bugmees. Little Critter's claim to fame and the popularity of Bugmees was due to the large number of bikers that stopped there on their weekend rides along the scenic country roads usually on their way up to Rabbit Hash or down toward Frankfort.

Coincidentally, when all the bikers started hanging out at Bugmees, the other two bars settled down and kept quiet. Though each one seemed overjoyed when an occasional biker would stop in for a drink. So now, things are rather peaceful in Little Critter.

Dandy, the owner of Bugmees was a biker and always helped support the local biker organizations. On most weekends he'd have burgers and hotdogs available with the beer the bikers bought on their pit stop along their ride. And, the bikers supported Dandy by stopping by on a regular basis.

The largest biker organization in the northern Kentucky area is Bike Riders of Kentucky, or BROK. Besides doing charity rides for various needy causes, BROK is full of men and women who just love to ride and do so at every opportunity. Every weekend you will see a bunch of them getting together for a ride along some of Kentucky's beautiful back roads, and often those rides have no destination at all in mind; it's just a ride for the fun of it.

It was a hot July Saturday when Black Jack Maxim, the first black man ever to be elected as president of BROK, was in the lead. Two-foot and Big M were following closely as they each navigated the curves and turns of the one lane country road. They had decided the day before to just; "go for a ride", No particular destination, no special time to get there or return. Their short ride had turned into a mile-eating venture as it often does with bikers.

They were about two hundred miles south of their usual stomping grounds in northern Kentucky, and were simply enjoying the ride. They came to a little town so small you'd better not blink or you'd miss it. It didn't even seem to have a name.

There was a small grocery store, a gas station, and a bar. Black Jack pulled into the bar parking lot. Big M pulled in right beside him, and Two-foot wheeled his trike around so he could back in. He liked to show off because his trike has "reverse" and the bikes didn't.

"I'm for washing some of the bugs out of my teeth, boys.", he announced.

"Sounds like a plan to me." said Big M as he and Two-foot followed him inside.

Inside the bar was dark enough they had to stop for a moment to let their eyes adjust. They sat down at the bar and Two-foot told the matronly-looking woman behind the bar;

"Three of your coldest beers, please." She smiled and reached into the cooler, while giving Black Jack a suspicious glance.

As they were drinking their second beer and talking about their ride, the barmaid came over to them again.

"Fellas, I don't want any trouble in here. There's a door in back by the toilets. You probably ought to go."

The three men looked at her in surprise, then turned as five of the local men entered.

"We're not looking for trouble either.", said Black Jack, "Why'd you say that?"

She didn't answer, but nodded toward the five men who were spreading out around the bar.

"You sure were right Jake; it is awful dark in here." one of the men announced loudly.

"Hellfire, Bubba," grinned another one, "Maybe we can lighten it up somewhat."

Black Jack groaned softly. "Shit! Guys," he said softly, " Looks like I'm gonna have to fight my way out of here."

"Hold on just a dammed minute, Bro." said Two-foot as he straightened up; "We came in together and we'll leave together! Besides, Partner ain't let me hit anybody in a long time."

Big M swiveled his bar stool around so he could face the local toughs. So did Two-foot and Black Jack.

"Me, I really don't want to fight anybody." he said with a slow shake of his head, "Cause every time I do I end up hurting somebody real bad."

"I want the biggest one!" whispered Two-foot.

"What the hell for?" asked Black Jack.

"Cause if I get whooped I can blame it on him being bigger than me." he grinned.

Black Jack and Big M both laughed. Then Big M said; "I'm ready when you are."

The other two men both nodded, then Black Jack suddenly yelled as loud as he could: "Charge!!"

And the three bikers left their stools in a flurry of swinging fists.

Caught off-guard the two rednecks that Black Jack and Big M had attacked went down and out, while Two-foot's opponent was backing up and trying to get away from the swinging beer-bottle Two-foot was trying to crush his skull with. The man had backed against the wall and raised his hands;

"Hey man!" he said with a pleading voice, "We was only jokin' really!" His two still standing friends were nodding their heads.

"Oh, okay." said Two-foot and seemed to relax, but when the man lowered his hands Two-foot brought the bottle down on his skull with a loud "thunk". The man sagged to the floor in a slump.

He held up the beer bottle and examined it closely.

"Damn!" said Two-foot disgustedly.

"What's up, Two-foot?" asked Black Jack. He wasn't even breathing hard. Two-foot showed him the bottle.

"It didn't even break, Bro." He said, then he stepped forward and swung it down on the fallen man's head again. Seeing the bottle was still intact he turned toward the two remaining new comers, one of who had picked up a cue stick.

"Hey Boy!" Big M growled at him; "You really need to put that stick down before someone sticks it up your ass! Sideways!"

The man quickly dropped the cue stick and backed up a couple more steps.

"Glad you butt-heads were jokin,", Two-foot said with a grin, "I want you to laugh this off!" He waved the bottle as he approached the other two men.

"Who's got the hardest head?"

"Hey, Two-foot," called Black Jack, "Leave 'em alone. Let's get out of here."

"Well, hell." grumbled Two-foot, "A man can't even have any fun around here."

Big M laid a twenty on the bar and nodded to the waitress; "Sorry about the disturbance ma'am."

Outside, the three men started their engines and were slowly pulling out of the parking lot. Just as they were about to pull onto the street a shot rang out and the bullet smashed Two-foot's windshield. Glancing back the bikers saw the man Big M had decked standing on the porch with a bloody face and a gun aimed in their direction.

"That red-neck sure is a slow learner!" Black Jack said as another bullet whizzed by them. He did a fierce, gravel-spitting "u" turn in the lot and faced the shooter. Left hand still holding his clutch, his right hand went behind his back and brought out the .38 he always carried. Three quick shots sent the local man back into the bar, and the three bikers sped off laughing.

"Damn," declared Big M, "I thought those days were over, Jack."

"Afraid not, Bro. The world is still full of fools!" said Two-foot as he fingered the hole in his windshield.

"See! That's why I'm always packin'," grinned Black Jack as he returned the firearm to its holster in the back of his pants. The three men gave out with a loud: "Eeeehaww!!" and started their way back home.

Two weeks later Black Jack led a small group of riders along the country road that ran peacefully past Little Critter. Most of the bikes were ridden by men with their wives sitting behind them. One bike however was ridden by Big M's wife; Short-stuff. She stood five-foot nothing, and was proud of the fact she could ride as good as most of the men. And better than some of them.

Black Jack didn't ride on past Little Critter, but pulled into the graveled parking lot of Bugmees. The riders with him did the same.

Black Jack was a large man, looking like he could have played professional football. But he had a quick and ready smile and an easy-going personality.

They had been riding for over an hour and it was time for some liquid refreshment. And to decide if they wanted to ride another thirty miles up to Rabbit Hash where they'd make another pit stop, or just travel some of the back roads for a while.

Rabbit Hash offered cold beer, a scenic overlook of the Ohio River, and practically zero interference from the citizens since the town consisted of a grocery store, a gift-souvenir store and a couple of nearby homes. The important thing to remember though is that the grocery store sold very cold beer and was always heavily stocked during the long riding season. It was one of the favorite stopping places for bikers from all over the area.

The back roads offered more riding and the joy of the wind in their hair, plus cold beer at any of the small bars that are scattered on almost every road in northern Kentucky. So it was a toss-up on which way they wanted to go, and they decided to hang out at Bugmees for a while and wash the bugs out of their teeth with some of Dandy's coldest bottled beverages of an alcoholic nature.

Maybe even toss down a few burgers and chips. About the only thing bikers like more than riding is eating and these boys…and girls…were past experts at both. Big M had been famous for single-handedly devouring two twenty-piece buckets of Colonel Sanders' famous recipe then eating two hamburgers with everything on 'em. Then he just laid down and took a nap.

Black Jack and his current woman, T.T.(short for Tiny Tits), were sitting at a table with Big M and Short-stuff when Dandy came over.

"Hey Jack, I heard you and Big M here and Two-foot had a bit of a run-in with some red-neck farm boys a couple of weeks ago. That right?"

"Hell, Bro," chuckled Black Jack, "It wasn't no big thing. Just some of those good ol' boys lookin' for fun in all the wrong places."

Big M nodded; "Yeah, there was only five of 'em, so us three had 'em out-numbered."

Short-stuff reached over and pinched M's cheek, turning his head toward her.

"Have you been fighting again? You promised me you'd stop all that fighting. Did you hurt anybody?" she asked angrily.

"Not much." Jack laughed, "The guy was able to get up and shoot at us."

"What!?" Short-stuff yelled; "You got shot at!?"

Big M looked at Black Jack and glared as Short-stuff's grip on his cheek tightened enough to leave a large red mark.

"You ain't helpin' matters Bro.", Big M grimaced painfully.

Dandy laughed at them and backed away.

"Hey, I didn't mean to start a family feud." He strolled back behind the bar.

Black Jack laughed too, then said to Big M:

"Hey M, remember how that peckerwood Two-foot was gonna hit with the bottle was shakin'?"

Big M slowly turned his face away from Short-stuff so her fingers slid off his cheek. He rubbed his cheek with a grimace.

"Yeah, that boy sure did have the tremors."

"Tremors Hell!" interrupted Two-foot, "That fool was shakin' like a dog shittin' a corn cob!"

The other three laughed a bit, then, Black Jack frowned at him.

"How the hell would you know something like that? You ever see a dog shit a corn cob?"

"Well," Two-foot nodded with a serious look, "Actually I have. See, I once owned this skinny, mangy weasely-lookin' dog named Obama. That dammed dog couldn't do anything right. You'd think he would have had some loyalty to me, to the one who took care of him and fed him and gave him a roof over his head, wouldn't ya?" He shook his head sadly, then, continued.

"But no, that dog would actually roam the other neighborhoods trying to get mongrel dogs to attack and bite me. He was sure a treasonous dog, Obama was. Anything I told him to do, he'd do right the opposite. So I finally figured out how to teach him a lesson."

Two-foot paused and took a drink of his beer. The other three waited for him to carry on.

"One day I took some old corn cobs and covered them with gravy and ex-lax. Then I sat them by the back door. Obama was out there watchin' me, so I yelled at him: 'leave this alone! Don't eat this!' And I went back into the house.

"Well, sure a shit stinks that bastard snuck up on the plate and ate all them corn cobs." Two-foot paused again and took another drink.

"Well, what happened?" Asked Short-stuff.

"Ahhh, it was funny as hell," Two-foot said with a grin. "A couple of hours later that dog was all hunched up and shakin' and tremblin' all over; tears were runnin' out of his eyes and he was just a-gruntin' and groanin'. Every time he'd pass one of them cobs he'd yelp in agony and try to bite his own ass. Then he'd begin to shakin' and shivverin' again. It was damn sure funny."

Black Jack chuckled, took a drink, then asked: "Whatever happened to the dog?"

"Oh man; this is the best part." Exclaimed Two-foot.

"One day some foreign-lookin' guy came by and saw Obama. He said the dog looked just like an egg-suckin' hound he owned back home, wherever that was, and wanted to know if he could buy him. So I told him if he promised to take Obama and his bitch and litter completely out of the country, he' could just have him. So he did."

The three other bikers sat looking at Two-foot for several seconds. Then Big M grunted:

"Bro, you're more full of crap that a chicken farm." And with that the four of them tipped their bottles again.

After a few hours and at least three 50-gallon trash cans full of empty beer bottles the BROK road captain, that huge ex-marine named Big M stood up and suggested they ride on up to Rabbit Hash so they could sit outside the store while drinking and watch the Ohio River as it meandered casually between Ohio and Kentucky.

The chapter treasurer, another ex-marine named Skidmark laughed and said: "Forget it Big M; you're so drunk you'd fall off your bike before we got half way there!" To which everyone laughed. Except Big M.

"Hey Bro," Big M growled; "I can out-ride you when I'm sound asleep!" Amid the cheering and jeering that erupted, Black Jack's ol' lady "T-T" stood up on a table and clapped her hands for attention.

"It looks to me like Big M and Skidmark are getting' ready to have a race. I'll bet an even hundred on Big M!" She declared while waving a fistful of money. The cheering was loud and the betting was heavy.

Big M's wife, Short-stuff punched him on the arm hard enough to raise a charley horse. "Don't do it!" she whispered gruffly in his ear, "You're too drunk. I don't wanna scrape you up off the pavement!"

"Aahhh Honey," he hiccupped, "I gotta do it. There's money on it. I can't back down." Having gone through this same scenario several times in the past Short-stuff knew she was fighting a losing battle.

"Okay Dummy," she said glaring at him, "But if you get killed I'm divorcing you!" Big M studied on it briefly, then responded: "Well, I guess I won't mind." He hugged her, kissed her and guffawed loudly when she bit his lip and kicked him on the shin.

"Hey Skidmark!" he yelled above the noise and confusion, "If you can find your bike let's go see if you know how to ride!" he began limping toward the door.

In a hurried fashion all the other bikers and their wives or girlfriends began tossing money on their tables to pay for their drinks, made their final bets on the race, and headed out the door to the parking lot.

Chapter Two

Billy Kirk once had the leading role in a low budget sci-fi TV. series called "Galactic Warriors". At an early age he had been diagnosed as a paranoid schizophrenic, but as long as he kept up with his medication he was able to function just about normally. Or at least as normal as anyone else in Hollywood. His weekly scripts dealing with strange worlds and aliens however, eventually caused his paranoia to grow even deeper and stronger.

He knew that the so-called E.T.'s and aliens he encountered each week in his series were just actors made up to look like beings from other worlds. But he started believing that the costumes and make-up they wore were based on true aliens from other planets that were being held captive someplace by some of the people who were out to get him.

His behavior became erratic; he was often late for work, missed his cues and once attacked a fellow actor who was made up as a Martian. His behavior eventually led to him getting fired from his show and the show itself being canceled.

Kirk had always been an avid reader, especially of things smacking of the occult and/or weird. He had once read the writings of the warrior-philosopher Walter Slovotsky who had written: "Relax, the universe really IS out to get you." That seemed to do it for Billy Kirk. He moped around for days arguing: how can you relax if the universe is out to get you? You have to fight back. In fact, you have to strike first whenever possible.

He had suspected for years the world was out to get him and this proved it to him. He sulked around his home for months trying to figure out a way to get even with all those he considered his enemies. And that was virtually everybody. He ignored his wife's efforts to encourage him and help him find other employment.

He would lock himself in his home office and spend hour after hour on the internet researching every thing he could think of that would give him the means for revenge. He even snuck back into the studio's warehouse one night and stole a couple of the fake ray guns they had used on his TV. series. He took them to a shady gun dealer who was well known in the ghetto for being able to make and or repair just about any type of firearm you could bring him.

Kirk told him what he wanted and left the guns with the man. He also left a thousand dollars, which was supposed to be a down payment for the job. When he returned a week later the gun dealer gave him back the plastic ray guns which he had simply turned into flashlights that lighted up when the trigger was pulled, told him there was no way anyone could make them real enough to shoot death rays, and told Kirk to get out of his store. He kept the thousand dollars "for his time and trouble"

Billy Kirk was beside himself in his fury over having been ripped off. But he was sane enough to know there wasn't much he could do about it. Actually, he thought, it was just another example of how the world was out to get him, and it made him even more determined to find a way to "get even".

He searched tirelessly for different chemical formulas that would allow him to create his own private army. Kirk knew he needed a huge army of people loyal to him if he hoped to take over the world, which he did indeed intend to do. Just how to get that army of loyal people was still the problem.

In one of his dope crazed research periods he came across an article about zombies. At first he just tossed it aside and thought nothing more about it. Zombies were the creation of Hollywierd. In several very old books, however, he discovered mention of zombies and of a formula that would turn normal people into those walking dead people that were almost invincible

It seems the gods of the dead finally smiled on his efforts though, for he heard about a well-known book collector who had recently died. The man's vast collection held numerous books and parchments that were hundreds of years old. All of books were being auctioned off to the highest bidder.

Kirk attended the auction, not really knowing what to expect. But when a set of ancient manuscripts came up for bids he simply couldn't help himself. He out bid everyone else and purchased the set for eleven thousand dollars.

At home he began to mentally berate himself for wasting the money when he needed it for his research. But he decided he might as well look over the manuscripts since they were now his.

In one hand-written manuscript over a hundred years old and penned in blood that was now so faded he could barely read it, he found reference to a chemical called Solanum that supposedly turned people into zombies. Seeing that the old manuscript had supposedly been written by a Haitian witch doctor seemed to give credibility to the writing.

By breaking down the chemicals described in the manuscript Kirk discovered that one of them had a modern equivalent called scopolamine, and another was identical to phenothiazine. The third ingredient was a mystery.

He knew the scopolamine could put a person into a hypnotic frame of mind, and the phenothiazine would make them docile. That could make them totally obedient to him, but he needed to know what that third chemical was that could make people almost invincible. He learned about trilomide a drug that made the patient totally pliable to suggestion. He experimented and kept researching.

Billy Kirk's wife was growing increasingly frustrated with his behavior, and had spoken to him about a trial separation. A couple of days later she mysteriously drowned in their home pool, though she was an excellent swimmer, and Billy found his troubles were over. He inherited all her money and now had the time and privacy to experiment as he wanted.

He began bringing prostitutes to his home drugging them and trying various experiments on them. He found he could make them do absolutely anything he wanted regardless of how perverted, how bizarre, or how painful it might be to them. They were mindless, totally obedient, but still destructible: they all died.

Disposing of the bodies was simple. Los Angeles has an uncounted number of alleys and vacant lots, many of which are in places considered by the police to be "high risk" areas of drugs and gang activities. Kirk was nearly killed himself one night while dumping his latest failed experiment.

He was pulling her body out of his trunk when he saw some members of the neighborhood gang approaching. Nighttime was a good time to dispose of bodies, but, Kirk realized, it was also a good time for gang-bangers and other villains to roam the streets looking for prey.

"Hey, white boy!" one of the bangers yelled as they continued in his direction, "What the hell you doin' on our turf?"

"Whatcha got there?" another one demanded.

"Damn! Look, it's a body!" the leader exclaimed.

For Billy Kirk, this called to mind another of Slovotsky's sayings: "Nothing's more annoying than somebody who had a keen eye for the obvious."

They were only about twenty yards away now, so he dropped the body, slammed the trunk and jumped in his car. As he was peeling out two or three, he never was sure, of the gang-bangers began firing at him. One of the bullets crashed through the rear window and then smashed through the windshield bare inches from his head. He drove through the wooden fence, bounced into the street and sped off.

Kirk waited nearly two weeks before taking his car to a garage for repair. He claimed he didn't know how the damage got there. The police took down the information, but told him it would be next to impossible to discover who did the damage. They advised him to file with his insurance company.

Kirk continued his research. But now he had to hide his failures in a different way. He was trying to be careful with the whores he brought home. He wasn't killing them just for sport, though he did admit it was a lot of fun and brought a certain kind of sexual pleasure they hadn't been able to provide while they were alive.

It was just that sometimes the things he made them do when under the spell of his drugs, and sometimes the way he treated them resulted in death.

He had made his basement into his lab and experiment room so that should he have any unexpected guests they would be unable to see what he was really doing. Down there he could lay out the bodies on a slanted table, drain the blood into buckets, then dismember the poor victim of his insanity. He put the dismembered body parts into plastic trash bags, weighted them down and carried them out to sea in his boat: "Slicin' n Dicin'". He dumped them off shore into the cold waters of the bay.

Several months passed and several more women died at his hands before he finally found what he was looking for. The correct mixture of drugs that made up the solanum he had read about. The unfortunate woman he had under his control at the time proved its efficiency. After subjecting her to various perversions to satisfy his own lust, Billy began cutting on her. The woman seemed to take no notice of the wounds. He used a fireplace poker to break one of her legs and she still struggled to move as he instructed her. She showed no signs of pain when he cut her breasts off either, though the blood flowed freely. The loss of blood seemed to have no effect on her. Kirk finally got his .38 special and shot her in the heart. She still did not die and continued to obey his every word.

Actually giggling with happiness William Kirk knew he had found the key to creating his army. He eventually killed the woman by crushing her skull with the poker.

He took her bagged body on a sea cruise and had her join the other women he had dumped there. Sixteen of them, if he remembered correctly. Counting the eleven or twelve (he couldn't remember which) bodies he had disposed of in various alleys and vacant lots Kirk realized he was making a pretty good start on ridding the world of people who were out to get him.

He felt he had truly found the correct formula that would help him create an army of zombies that would be totally and completely obedient to him, and would help him take over the world. Still; there was at least one more experiment he had to make.

It was a Friday evening and he knew the prostitutes would be out in droves. He cruised down Forest Avenue, one of their popular money--making hangouts. He was so excited he already had an erection, but sex wasn't the object of this evening's venture. Spotting a group of four women in very tight, very short hot pants and practically topless, he pulled over to the curb.

"Hi Honey," smiled a tall blond as she approached the car, "You lookin' for a date?"

Kirk had a wad of money in his hand and deliberately let the woman see several hundred - dollar bills.

"Yes, I am." He answered with his own smile, "But I want something special…and I'm willing to pay."

The woman opened the door and slid into the seat beside him.

"Honey, everything I do is special. You just let me know what you want and I'll tell you how much. Then we can concentrate on seeing how good I can make you feel." She casually reached over and ran her long fingernails across the bulge in his trousers.

A delicious shiver ran up his spine, and his mouth was getting dry.

"How much for you to pick a friend and the two of you spend the rest of the night with me?" He nodded to the other three women standing in a huddle several feet away watching the traffic pass by.

"Sweetheart," the blond smiled, "as handsome as you are, we'll give you a special rate." She turned to the open window and called out: "Mona, come here."

A somewhat shorter brunet sauntered over with an exaggerated sway of her hips. The blond turned back to Kirk, "Honey, my name is Sugar, and I promise you'll say I'm the sweetest thing you ever had. Me and Mona will have you climbing the walls and begging for mercy." She opened the door and motioned for Mona to get in beside her.

"Mona, this nice handsome man is going to buy our services for the remainder of the night. I told him we'll give him a special rate of only $1,500.00. That sound okay with you?" Mona's eyes widened in surprise, but she quickly recovered, "Well, I suppose so Sister. I don't mind giving a discount for a man as nice looking as this one. What's your name Sweetie?"

Having been down this road numerous times before, Kirk was ready with his response.

"I'm Jackson Carter. I just bought a place over on the coast, and I'm hornier than a herd of long-horn steers!"

Sugar giggled gaily and fondled his crotch again. "Ohh Baby, I'm sure we can take care of all that!"

The drive back to his house was passed in non-sense chatter as he continued to tell them how much he wanted them, and hint at all the sexual things he wanted them to do with him, and each other. To further put them at ease, he handed Sugar the wad of cash.

"Guess you ladies want your money up front, right?" The money quickly disappeared down Sugar's top, secured safely (she thought) between her size 38 breasts.

How stupid they are, Kirk thought to himself. And how easy to fool. Ohh, he fully intended to exhaust himself in a sexual orgy with them, but after that would come time for his final experiment. He smiled to himself as he pictured the surprise and fear they would display. He certainly wasn't worried about the money, he would simply retrieve it from Sugar's dead body.

He pulled into his driveway and they all got out.

"Come on in, ladies, there's champagne and party-time just waiting for us!" Both women laughed merrily and followed him in.

"This is the living room, girls," Kirk announced, "I'll put on some music, and pour us some refreshment while you two get naked for me. I figured we could start here and just work our way into the bedroom."

Both women giggled and began stripping.

Handing them each a glass, Kirk slowly removed his own clothing as his eyes traveled over the exposed, inviting bodies of the two women. Both were well-endowed in their breasts, and while Sugar's waist narrowed down then filled out in a wide display of hips, Mona's waist was a bit chubbier, but still very sexy.

As his pants fell to the floor, Mona gasped in fake alarm: "Oh Baby, I don't know if I can take all that. You'll have to be careful with me at first." He mentally laughed at her poor attempt at innocence.

"Well, we'll just have to take it one step…I mean one inch at a time, won't we?" he said with a leer.

"Drink up ladies, there's plenty more where that came from."

Sugar finished off her drink, then knelt in front of him.

Billy Kirk stood with his feet spread as she began to pleasure him. He watched as Mona finished her drink and set the glass down on the coffee table. He motioned for her to approach and when she did he began fondling her breasts.

She closed her eyes and moaned in pleasure, though Kirk was certain it was pretend. Suddenly Sugar stopped her ministrations and just knelt there in front of him.

He touched her on the side of the head and said hoarsely; “Keep sucking.”, and she began again.

Her rhythm was different, and she was obviously a bit clumsier than she had been, and he knew the drug had taken effect.

Turning his attention back to Mona he saw that she was now just standing there with her eyes closed. He pinched one of her nipples as hard as he could. She showed no awareness of the pain. He smiled to himself and muttered; “Let the games begin.” Reaching down he finished himself off in Sugar’s mouth.

Several hours later, after he had fulfilled every sexual fantasy he had ever had, Billy Kirk ordered the two women to follow him down into the basement. He had Mona lie down on his “operating” table. He pushed the button that raised the foot of the table about two feet, placed a bucket under her head, and ordered Sugar to cut Mona’s throat, and giggled at her quick, though clumsy obedience.

As the blood drained from her body, Kirk told Sugar to bite off one of Mona’s nipples. She did so without hesitation. He had her swallow it. The absolute power he had, the total control over them he now had gave him the strongest erection he had ever had.

Bending Sugar over the table so that her face was in Mona's crotch, he relieved himself wildly and violently in her backside. As he exploded in her, he was gasping for breath. He withdrew from her and sagged to his knees, his face resting against her buttocks as he tried to regain his breathing.

Finally he stood, saw that Mona had stopped bleeding, and told Sugar to sit down on the floor. She obeyed without sound or protest. He too, sat down and waited, watching Mona anxiously.

After a few moments he noticed a slight movement of Mona's right hand.

"Mona," he said in an authoritative voice; "Get up and go over to Sugar. Bite her on the shoulder as hard as you can."

He knew that Mona was dead, but now was some how re-animated by his formula. He watched as she bit a chunk out of Sugar's shoulder and ate it. Sugar sat motionless. While he knew Sugar was totally under his command, she was still alive. And, therefore still vulnerable and unfit to be in his army.

In about fifteen minutes Sugar fell over onto her side. He felt her pulse and saw that it was quickly growing weaker. Kirk went to his workbench and picked up a pistol. He shot Sugar in the heart. Then he sat down to wait.

In less than ten minutes he saw a slight stirring of her limbs.

"Sugar, get up." He ordered. She did so awkwardly. Kirk's joy was beyond description. He knew he had what he needed to put his world-domination plan into effect. His drug not only turned people into zombies, but it was easily passed from one person to another with a bite. Just like in all those stupid movies he used to make fun of.

Both women were absolutely dead, and yet they were totally under his command. They couldn't be killed again, except by destroying their brains.

He turned his cameras on and filmed them as they used the knives he'd given them to hack and stab at each other according to his instructions. When he grew tired of his sport he shot each of them in the head, dismembered the bodies, and later took them out to sea and dumped them.

Although crazy in every legal and medical sense of the word Billy Kirk was clever enough to know he needed a place of privacy to begin his army and implement his take -over of the world. He began selling off all his cars and real estate. Including the mansion his late wife had left him, and his boat; "Slicin' n Dicin'"

Within a few weeks he liquidated all his assets and moved out of his Hollywood mansion. He bought a small farm that had several out buildings and was located about three hundred yards off the highway. Kirk had the moving company haul all his remaining possessions to his new residence. The farm happened to be in a small community known as Little Critter, Kentucky.

Chapter Three

Dandy strolled over to where Big M was about to straddle his bike.

"Hey M, I hear you collect swords and knives and all that kinda stuff."

Before M could say anything Short-stuff piped up:

"Collect hell! He amasses that crap by the truck load!" she stated with a smile.

"Well, yeah: I do have a few swords…maybe twenty or twenty-five that I've collected over the years. And probably three or four hundred hunting knives, bowie knives, and such."

"And that's not counting the two or three hundred pocket knives he has!" declared Short-stuff, "He keeps on collecting that stuff we're gonna have to build on another room to the house."

"My brother-in-law does a lot of flea markets, gun and knife shows and stuff like that." Dandy replied, "He's gonna be here this afternoon with a bunch of his swords and knives, maybe a few guns. Why don't you bring your stuff and maybe you two could do some swapping?"

"Sounds like a plan to me." Big M answered. He pulled out his cell phone, "I'll call my daughter and have her load them up and drive them over in her car. Right now me and

Skidmark have a race to run. I'll be back in three or four hours."

"Hell, it'll take you that long just to find Rabbit Hash!" joked Cruiser as he stumbled over to his own bike.

"Skidmark grinned and nodded toward Cruiser, "That boy thinks he's slicker than snot on a doorknob, but really you could sand the paint off jail house wall with him!"

Dandy surveyed the cheerful fun-loving crowd of bikers with a concerned eye. They had finished off over twenty cases of beer. That was nearly two cases each, and they were showing the effects of the alcohol. They were bikers, known for hard drinking and hard riding, but they were also his friends and he was worried.

"Do you know if Two-foot's gonna be here?" Dandy asked, "He's supposed to be bringing the latest edition of the Road Wheeler."

Two-foot was actually five foot five, but was the shortest man in the crowd . Even most of the women were taller than he was, so naturally everybody had to give him a lot of crap about his size.

When one of the other bikers joked him about his size, Two-foot would usually say: "Hey Bro, it ain't easy being me, but no one else wanted the job, so I'm stuck with it," He also wrote for the local biker magazine called The Road Wheeler, and was the magazine's delivery person for the area. His main claim to fame however, was that he admitted to being an incorrigible, un-repentant smart aleck.

Cowboy's bike was parked beside Big M's and when he overheard Dandy's question he responded: "Two-foot? Yeah I saw him back at the BP station. We were both getting' gas and he said he had one more stop to make before he'd be here."

"He ridin' that home-made trike of his?" Dandy asked.

"Of course," said Short-stuff, grinning, "He never misses a chance to go for a ride."

"Hey Big M!" shouted Skidmark from across the parking lot; "You passed out over there or somethin'? Thought we had us a race to go to"

"Semper fi, mother lover!" hollered Big M back at him, "Crank 'er up. I'm ready!"

"Hey, hey," shouted T.T. "Let's get 'er done!"

Chapter Four

After having dined in all the most famous restaurants in Hollywood Kirk found the simple country fare of Little Critter barely eatable. "But one has to eat, doesn't one?" he said to himself as he seated himself at a red and white checkered Formica table in a back corner of the Hog Jowl Inn.

The waitress that brought his order was friendly enough, and Kirk was surprised to notice she seemed to have all her teeth. He had heard lots of jokes about the men and women in Kentucky having only one or two teeth in their mouths.

He chuckled silently to himself as he wondered if it was true that there was a lot of in-breeding in Kentucky. He'd heard that so much incest was going on that there was probably only seven or eight different DNA patterns in all the population.

Looking around at the half-filled café, he saw several of the local women, mostly younger ones, but a couple in their mid-to-late forties.

"Damn!" he thought to himself, "Look at all those fine asses. I wouldn't mind breeding with some of them myself." Feeling that old familiar tingle in his groin, Kirk forced his mind back to his meal.

He nerved himself and cut into his chicken fried steak with white gravy, which was the specialty of the inn. Chewing slowly and trying to pretend he was at the Brown Derby in Hollywood he looked up to see a man approaching him with a big grin on his face.

"I know you!" the man declared, "You that actor fella…uhh…uhh Kirk, right? Billy Kirk. I used to watch all them there programs of yours. They was really cool, all about space monsters and such."

Kirk was about to tell the man to shove off when he noticed that man's uniform. According to the badge on his shirt his name was Jemson. The shirt was brown and had "Critterden City Jail" sewed on it in fancy embroidery. Billy Kirk's brain kicked into overdrive and he suddenly knew where he was going to get his army. He stood and offered his hand.

"Won't you join me Mr. Jemson?"

"Ahh shucks Mr. Kirk. You can just call me Leroy." He sat down and when the waitress came over said:

"Hannah, bring me one of yer rancher omelets and a pot of coffee. And put Mr. Kirk's meal on my tab, would ya?"

Trying not to be obvious, Kirk watched Hannah's backside as she walked away. Once more he felt that tingle in his boxers, and had to force his mind back to the conversation he was having with Mr. Jemson.

During that meal and several others in the following days Kirk was able to find out from the friendly guard the jail routine, the number of prisoners, how many were felons facing probable prison time, and how many were simple misdemeanors. He also learned how many guards were on at any given time. He carefully filed all this information away in his paranoid mind and began devising his plan.

He contacted some of the people he had once dealt with for various not-so-legal substances and placed his order. He knew he would be notified as soon as the items were available and he paid for them.

In the days while he waited for that notification he carefully boarded up all the windows and doors of the huge barn on his new property. He left only one door operable; one that he could see easily from his house a few yards away.

A week later his shipment arrived and he began preparing his formula of solanum. He had previously purchased several cases of cheap wine. With a hypodermic needle he injected each bottle with enough solanum to affect several people.

He also injected enough arsenic into each bottle to kill at least a dozen people. "The arsenic will kill them," he grinned to himself,

"And the solanum bring them back to ….well, kind of life. Life enough to serve as my army, anyway."

He stored the bottles of wine in the barn along with several blankets. As he worked with the bottles of wine, he sang his own words to an early Frank Sinatra song: "I'm gonna take over the world, and I'll do it my way." He laughed.

It was a Friday evening and Kirk dressed himself all in black. "After all," he though with an insidious grin, "isn't that the way secret agents and assassins dress?" He knew that tonight the security at the jail would be at it's lowest. There would be only two guards on duty, the others would be home resting and getting rested up for the following day when the inmates were allowed visitors. Saturdays were always hectic and extra guards were always on hand in case of trouble.

It was a few minutes to midnight when he shoved the nine-millimeter in his waistband, picked up his uzi, and walked out the door. His black four-wheel drive Blazer got him to the parking lot behind the jail in fifteen minutes. He parked beside one of the jail's transport buses.

He sat silently for a few minutes contemplating his plan. He knew he was about to make a move that would change his life forever. "Yeah," he whispered to himself, "and the lives of all those fools who are trying to get me."

He fumbled in the glove box and pulled out a bag of pills. He swallowed three of them without water, shuddered as they went down. He sat for a few minutes while the pills took effect, then got out of the car and approached the rear entrance of the jail. He was almost bouncing on the balls of his feet.

Billy Kirk was high and he knew it. But he was not careless. Aware that the world was out to get him, he knew he had to be very careful not to tip anyone off that he was aware of their conspiracy. And that he was going to get them first.

As he glanced around to make sure no one was taking a midnight stroll nearby he banged loudly on the door. After a moment he banged again and continued until he heard keys rattling on the other side of the door.

He stepped back as the door swung open. It was Officer Jemson, as he knew it would be.

"What the hell…why Mr. Kirk, what you doin' our here this time o' night?" He had his hand resting on his holstered service revolver, but did not pull it out.

"LeRoy, let me in. It's an emergency!" Kirk gasped in apparent distress.

"Sure thing Mr. Kirk. What's the problem?" he asked as he stepped aside to let Kirk in. He was about to relock the door when Kirk pulled his pistol and shot him in the back of the head. Quickly he ran down the long quiet corridor toward the jail's control center where he knew the other guard would be. His rubber-soled shoes made hardly a sound as he ran.

Kirk was almost at the end of that corridor when he heard the sound of jangling keys and hurried footsteps. He stopped and pressed himself against the wall while trying to quiet his breathing. As the guard came around the corner Kirk slammed his pistol into the man's face.

The guard dropped with only a grunt and Kirk bent down to grab his gun. He stood up smiling. It would take the guard a minute or two to regain his senses and Kirk smiled with satisfaction as he figured everything was going according to plan. He removed the guard's handcuffs and locked the man's hands behind his back just as he moaned and tried to get up.

As the guard struggled to sit up, Kirk kicked him in the stomach.

"Shut up and be still!" he ordered gruffly, "You better do exactly everything I tell you to do or I will splatter your stupid civil servant brains all over this place! Do you understand!?"

The guard was alert now and beginning to realize how precarious his situation was.

"Yes…yes I understand. What do you want?"

"Get up!" Kirk said and helped him to his feet. "Take me to the control room". He noticed the guard trying to look around, and he giggled;

"If you're hoping for help from Jemson, forget it. He's laying dead by the back door."

The guard, a Critterden native named Roscoe Havens began trembling inside. He knew he was in a deep pile of something that didn't smell like fresh coffee. He determined to be as cooperative as possible while looking for an opportunity to escape.

"Show me on the roster which cells the felons are in." Kirk demanded.

Havens did exactly that and showed Kirk where the keys to those cells were hanging on the wall, telling him that the felons were kept on the first floor so they could be watched more closely.

Billy Kirk grinned delightedly all the while congratulating himself on his brilliant plan. He ordered Officer Havens out of the control room and marched him down the main corridor until they were standing between the two banks of cells. There were twenty-five single man cells of each side of the corridor and most were occupied.

The cell house was quiet in the way only a huge steel and stone building can be quiet. Except for an occasional snore the place seemed deserted.

"Sit your ass down on the floor." Kirk told the guard, and smiled again at the instant obedience. He took a deep breath and shouted as loudly as he could.

"Wake up boys! Wake up and meet your new destiny!"

There were sounds of cursing and grumbling as several men got out of their cots and came to their cell doors.

"Shut the hell up mister!" a large tattooed man told Kirk, "Who the hell you think you are anyway?"

Kirk gave him a smile and a casual salute with his gun.

"I'm the man who can get you out of here and into a place where you can make more money and have more freedom than you ever dreamed." he replied.

"Yeah, that's what you say!" said an inmate through the bars of his cell door on the other side of the corridor.

"Listen to me everybody!" Kirk shouted again, "I need some men to help me pull a job that will bring in over six hundred million dollars. I can get you out of here right this minute if you want to join me. When the job is finished you can remain with me or head off on your own. But if you join me right now I demand and expect total obedience to every order I give you until the job is complete." He placed his foot against the side of the guard's face and shoved him over.

"Watch this!" he yelled at the inmates. He pointed his gun at the guard and shot him in the head. The shot echoed and re-echoed off the concrete walls.

"That lets you know I am serious. If you join me you'll be living a life of luxury, but if you cross me in any way I'll kill you. Now that you know the score how many of you want to join me?"

It was totally silent for a moment as the imprisoned men digested what they had just witnessed, then several stuck their arms through their bars and waved.

"I'm in!"

"Me too! Let me outta here."

"I'm yer huckleberry!" shouted another.

Kirk giggled and began unlocking cell doors. The big tattooed man stepped out and faced Kirk.

"They call me Bigfoot. I'll be your second in command if you'll let me. I love your style."

Kirk handed him the remaining keys. "You're hired. Let the rest of them out."

One of the newly freed men went over to the dead guard and pulled out his wallet.

"Leave it.", Kirk told him, "In two days you'll have more money than you've ever seen."

"Okay, but what'll we do before those two days?"

Billy Kirk looked at him intently for a moment, then responded, "That's a good question. And the answer is that you will all be staying in my place for two days until the heat from your escape dies down a little. It's just a big barn-like structure but you'll be out of sight and comfortable with plenty to eat and drink."

A skinny guy with red splotches on his face grinned and slapped the first man on the back.

"Hell's bells Tony, I'm likin' this better and better the more I hear."

Bigfoot approached with three more men. Kirk could see a man waving further down the cellblock and yelling to be let out.

"Why didn't you let him out?" he questioned Bigfoot.

"The dude's a friggin' snitch!" Bigfoot declared, "He can't be trusted."

"Is that right?" Kirk asked softly. He handed Bigfoot the pistol but as he did so he allowed his jacket to open so they could all see the uzi hanging from his shoulder. "Show me I can trust you. Go kill him."

"Ahh shit." The big man exclaimed, "I been wantin' to do that for weeks."

Kirk and all the other eighteen men watched silently as Bigfoot walked purposefully down to the man's cell.

"Let me out Bigfoot. I wanna go too." the man said.

"Okay snitch, yer out." Bigfoot said and shot him between the eyes. He came back to Kirk and offered him the gun. Kirk realized he did indeed have a second in command he could trust. A little bit.

"Keep it.", he told the big man. He turned to the group of restless inmates.

"Are those cameras recording anything?" Kirk asked Bigfoot.

"No. They just make it easy for the guards to watch what's goin' on in the cell blocks."

"Ok. There's one of the jail transport buses out back. You'll all get in it and follow me back to my place. Bigfoot will appoint one of you to drive. It's only a short drive so don't try to speed or do anything else stupid."

Bigfoot waved the gun. "You heard the boss, boys. Let's go. JoJo , grab the keys out of the control room. You drive."

Kirk stood by his car while the just-released jail -birds boarded the bus. When he heard the bus motor roar to life with a cough and a sputter he got in his car and backed out, then waited for the bus to do the same.

Several uneventful minutes later Kirk stopped beside the huge barn on his farm. He got out of his car and opened the barn door motioning for JoJo to drive on in. He watched the men exit the bus and begin milling around inside the barn.

"Look over there by the wall." He told them, "There's enough wine for you to celebrate your new freedom. There's blankets to wrap up in for tonight. Tomorrow I'll arrange for food and better lodgings."

There was a mad scramble for the bottles of wine. JoJo tossed one to Bigfoot and Kirk motioned the big man over.

"Bigfoot, I know you have to sleep some time too, so I'm going to lock this door for tonight. Make sure you keep that gun with you."

"Sure thing Boss." The tattooed man nodded, "You can count on me." He nodded again as he took a small drink of the wine.

"See you boys in the morning!" Kirk said loudly. He stepped out and locked the barn door.

He hurried back to the house with an erection so hard he was in pain. He was a genius and he knew it. His plan was falling into place and soon his army of nineteen men would grow and continue to grow until he could take over the whole country. Then the world.

Sitting naked on the side of his bed Kirk took matters in hand while thinking of the fun he would have as Boss of the World.

Chapter Five

As the BROK members were laughing and joking with each other they lined their bikes up on each side of the parking lot. This left a wide pathway down the middle where Big M and Skidmark would drive through before hitting the main road and throttling down for the actual race.

Black Jack always carried a snub-nosed .38 special with him. He was a big friendly black man who tried to get along with everybody. But he had in times past been in a couple of situations down in redneck country where that .38 was the only thing that kept him alive.

Just recently he had been with Big M and Two-foot when the three of them got into a little fracas down south with some of the local rednecks.

A lot of the off-the-beaten-path little towns and villages in Kentucky still had their fair share of Klansmen, and Black Jack had learned not to take chances. He held the gun up pointing toward the sky.

"You butt-heads ready!?", he asked. Big M yelled: "Ready to kick some butt!" as Short-stuff kissed him on the cheek.

Just then the sound of another motor caught their attention and everyone turned toward the road as Two-foot wheeled in on his trike.

"What's up guys?" he asked. T-T ran over and gave him a hug, almost poking him in the eye with one of her nipples as her tank top had a wardrobe malfunction. She giggled and covered herself.

"Gee, Two-foot, I must be gladder to see you than I thought."

"T.T., I shore am glad to see …eh, you too." Two-foot stammered as she turned and hurried back to Black Jack.

"Big M and Skidmark are having a race up to Rabbit Hash.", she called over her shoulder.

"Yeah, so get your trike outta the way!" yelled Cruiser. Two-foot pulled on over to the side and got off his trike.

Digging into his tour pack he pulled out two bundles of magazines. "Hey guys, I've got the new Road Wheeler here."

"Gimme one," said Short-stuff, "It'll give me something to do while M is off playing Evel Knievel."

Two-foot carried the two bundles over to the picnic table and laid them down, then cut the binding straps. Several hands reached for the magazine, and he stood back out of the way.

"You got a poem in this one?" asked Cowboy.

"Of course. I always do." answered Two-foot, " It gives me a chance to express my literary talent."

"Well express your literary talent by getting your trike out of the way!" yelled Black Jack

"That ain't no trike, it's a bike with training wheels!" laughed Baby Hoss' wife Bow-legged Sally.

"Wait a minute Black Jack." Hollered Skidmark, "Big M got a kiss on the cheek for luck, that ain't fair."

"Ahh hell Bro." laughed Two-foot as he hurried over to Skidmark. He kissed him on the cheek "You know I luvs ya boy!" he said with another laugh. The crowd cheered and Skidmark turned red but laughed too.

"You white boys gonna race or not!?", shouted Black Jack.

"I'm ready now." declared Skidmark.

"Me too!" agreed Big M.

Black Jack again raised his gun preparing to fire the starting shot. Again however, he was stopped. This time by Dandy hurrying out of the bar with his cell phone held to his ear and waving his other hand for attention.

"Hey guys, hold on a minute!" he shouted. He paused while listening to his phone, then shook his head and put the phone in his pocket.

"That was Sheriff Taylor. There's been a jailbreak and all the guys in there with felony charges against them, have escaped. There were two guards killed and one inmate. He wants us to be on the look- out. He said he thinks nineteen guys escaped."

Dandy was breathless after relating this news and stopped to catch his breath.

"How the hell could nineteen dudes escape from the jail?" asked Cruiser while trying to get back off his bike. "Where the hell did they get a gun?"

"When did it happen?" asked T-T

"Sometime last night he thinks." answered Dandy. "They stole the jail transport bus and drove away but nobody saw which direction they went. They could be a hundred miles from here by now, or hiding in somebody's back yard or something."

"They'll be easy to spot wearin' those stupid orange jump suits." Two-foot chimed in.

"Yeah, that's right. So if we see anybody with an orange jump suit on do we make a citizen's arrest or something?" asked Skidmark.

"Hell no," declared Dandy, "Call 911 and get the police. Some of those guys are pretty dangerous. They done killed two guards."

"Hell Dandy, I ain't worried," laughed Two-foot as he put his arm around Big M, "I've got the U.S. Marines on my side. I'll just sic Big M and Skidmark on 'em.", he shook his head thoughtfully.

"I'd just like to know how they did it." he continued with a grin, "I coulda sure used that information once upon a time."

Several of the bikers laughed for they knew Two-foot had once served prison time, and more than one of them had been a jail a few times for being drunk in public, fighting, or otherwise disturbing the peace at different times in their lives.

"Hell yes," chimed in Jynx, "knowin' how to escape from jail is some good information to have."

Black Jack motioned for everyone to gather in. Bikes were turned off and the biker men and women got off and approached him.

"I don't think we got anything to worry about, but what ya all say? Wanna still ride, or what?"

Just then a car pulled into the parking lot and Big M said: "There's Maggie with my hardware."

Many of the bikers had seen Big M's collection of swords and knives before, but were always ready to look again. Most of them carried a boot-knife of some kind. As they gathered around Maggie's car M pulled out a blanket-wrapped bundle and laid it on a nearby picnic table. He carefully unrolled the bundle and displayed a variety of swords and bowie knives.

"I didn't bring all of them, Dad," said Maggie, "Just the ones from the wall with the window."

"That's okay, Hon," responded Big M as he hugged her, "This'll be enough to start with."

Several of the men began helping Big M carry the weapons inside the bar. The men pulled a couple of tables together to lay the items on, and watched as Big M spread them out and arranged them for easy inspection.

"Good grief, Big M" exclaimed Cowboy, "You got enough blades here to take on all the ninjas in China!"

As they were studying with appreciation the vast collection they were interrupted by the sound of brakes screeching . They turned quickly toward the highway and watched as a large Ford pick-up with a bed cap on it pulled into the parking lot.

"That's my brother-in-law!" announced Dandy, "He always drives like a dammed Yankee!" The pick-up pulled alongside the bar and stopped. A short, very over weight man got out as most of the bikers approached him.

"Shit, Dandy," grinned Two-foot, "I like him already; he's shorter than me."

The man apparently heard Two-foot's remark because he paused and looked at the vertically challenged biker.

"Shorter than you!" he exclaimed, "Bullshit! You're short enough to sit on the edge of a cigarette paper and swing your legs." He gave a huge grin at his smart remark.

Two-foot didn't miss a step.

"Shit! You're short enough to walk under a snake's belly with a top-hat on!" Both men laughed as did several of the other bikers.

Dandy and the man shook hands warmly and Dandy turned to the crowd;

"This is Hank. Couple of you help him take his stuff inside so him and Big M can check each other out."

Hank opened the tail- gate of the truck. The back of the truck was piled high with various swords, long-bladed knives, and several pistols all in display cases. Hank backed away, but stood near-by so he could keep an eye on things.

"Come inside and get a beer, Hank." said Dandy as he put his arm around Hank's shoulder and led him toward the door.

"You can trust these guys. They're my friends, and I guarantee you they'll never do you wrong unless you do them wrong first."

Hank chuckled softly, and said: "Only a dammed fool would do a bunch of bikers wrong. And I ain't no fool."

Dandy squeezed his shoulder affectionately; "No, but you're a Yankee, and that's almost as bad."

"Okay, Brother, I'll take your word for it." responded Hank. As they walked toward the tavern's doorway, Hank slapped Dandy on the back and grinned. "I saw your girlfriend this morning." he said, "Man, that one tooth she's got sure is pretty!" he laughed loudly at his own joke. Dandy just shook his head.

Cowboy and Baby Hoss and Cruiser had their arms full of display cases and followed them inside. Two-foot held the door open as Skidmark and Jynx entered with their arms full.

In a few moments, all of Big M's and Hank's wares were laid out on tables and the men were gathering around to look and comment. Dandy strolled over and Hank looked up at him with a silly grin.

"Dandy, do you know what the definition of foreplay is in Kentucky?" he waited expectantly for Dandy to respond.

"No, but I'm sure you'll tell me."

"Yeah," Hank chuckled, "In Kentucky foreplay is: Hey Sis, turn off the lights." Again he laughed at his own attempt at humor.

Two-foot faced him across the table, "Well just remember, Yankee-boy, you're in Kentucky now, and you're way out-numbered. You might not make it back across the river." He said it with a smile and laugh, but Hank saw that his eyes weren't smiling.

Hank lowered his head and began examining Big M's swords.

Most of the women had sat at another table and were chatting amongst themselves.

"Must be a man-thing." said Cowboy's wife Peanuts, "I could understand it if they were getting all ga-ga over shoes or jewelry, or something like that. But knives and swords!?"

The women laughed and agreed with her, though most of them also had a knife of some kind in her purse or pocket.

"It's not just a man-thing," said Short-stuff, "It's a matter of little boys and their toys." They all laughed again as Sandy, Dandy's only barmaid, brought over a tray of beers for them.

"Can one of you ladies kinda keep an eye on the parking lot. I know most of those weapons of Hank's are legal, but not all of them. And from what I've seen of M's, I know we don't want the wrong people to walk in on us."

"Not a problem, Dandy." said Short-stuff. "We'll take our beer and sit at the picnic table outside. Can you cook me up a hamburger?"

"Yeah, me too." Said Bow-legged Sally, "I'm feelin' a bit dizzy. Need something to settle my stomach."

"Honey," said Peanuts with a grin, "Baby Hoss said if you ever got dizzy it would be an improvement."

"Screw you too," laughed Sally as she staggered toward the door behind Short-stuff.

Black Jack and Two-foot saw what the women were doing, and nodded their approval.

Chapter Six

Kirk awoke with a feeling of exhilaration. Today, if everything went alright last night, the escaped prisoners in his barn should all be unconscious and ready to receive their orders. Ready to become the first squad of his invincible army. They wouldn't have weapons because they wouldn't be coordinated enough to use them. But they needed no weapons. He would order them to kill and bite everyone they met, for everyone they bit would within a few short minutes become zombies just like them and soon he would have a vast army ready to take over the town.

Then the adjoining town, then the state, then…then… He giggled to himself as he felt another erection, and he debated whether or not to take care of it. He groped himself a moment or two, then suddenly decided it would have to wait. He needed to check on his prisoners. "I mean, my army.", he corrected himself.

He quickly dressed, ate a hurried breakfast of Froot Loops with chocolate chip cookies crumbled in with it, grabbed the uzi and headed out the door toward the barn. He was about to unlock the barn door when his paranoia hit him again. He eased around the side of the barn to where there was a knothole about the size of golf ball. He stooped down and peered in.

It was light enough Kirk could see that everyone was laying down in various poses of deep sleep. Except Bigfoot and JoJo. Those two were stationed on either side of the barn door, Bigfoot with the pistol ready and pointing at the door, and JoJo with a length of 2 by 4. He moved back in front of the door and called: "Hey Bigfoot, everybody ready to go?", then hurried back to his peephole.

He saw Bigfoot crouch down and aim determinedly at the door as he responded: "Yeah, Boss man. Everybody's ready to see what your plans are so we can make some of that big money you were talkin' about." JoJo was shifting his make shift bat around like he was stepping up to the plate for the first pitch.

Billy Kirk sighed to himself: "Always complications!" he thought to himself. Then chuckled as he poked the barrel of his uzi through the knothole aimed toward the two criminals. Before he could fire, though, Bigfoot noticed it and yelled at JoJo; "Get down! The bastard's tryin' to kill us!" He dove to the side and fired at Kirk through the barn wall. Kirk was splattered with several splinters of wood that stabbed into his right cheek and neck as he pulled the trigger.

The uzi burped and sprayed instant death into the barn. Except there was no one to receive that death sentence. Bigfoot had rolled to the side and was hiding behind the transport bus and was firing at where he figured Kirk had to be. And

JoJo had dove behind a stack of hay bales where he moaned and cursed Kirk in his fear.

"Don't know what the hell your trip is Boss-man," Bigfoot yelled out, "but you've got all these guys knocked out. Me and JoJo woulda been too if we hadn't been doin' somethin' else instead of drinkin' that crap you had in here! What the hell's goin' on anyway?"

Kirk had run several feet away from the barn and was trying to calm his adrenalin-fed heart. The fear of almost getting shot had scared the shit out of him and he could prove it: it was still running down his leg. He screamed his rage and fear and peppered the barn door with burst after burst from the hot-barreled uzi until he ran out of bullets.

"You should have drunk too, Bigfoot. Now I'm going to have to shoot you!", he screamed.

He started back toward the house, then paused. Bigfoot could get away by driving the bus through the door. That simply wouldn't do at all, Kirk thought. He had to figure a way to stop that from happening.

Returning to his knothole, he took a quick peek inside. He couldn't see JoJo, but he could see Bigfoot as he knelt beside the bus looking all around trying to see where Kirk might be.

"Hey Boss man," Bigfoot yelled, "Just tell me what's going on. Maybe I'll still wanna help you!"

Kirk eased the barrel of the uzi part way through the knothole, aimed in the direction of the front of the bus and pulled the trigger trying to spray the motor with hot lead. Again two bullets crashed through the aged barn wood and nearly hit him.

He nearly dropped his weapon as he jumped away from the barn. He was breathing heavily and could still smell the mess in his pants. He knew no one could see him, still he was totally humiliated.

Growling and cursing in his paranoid anger he hurried back to the house. He wanted to get more bullets. And he wanted to wipe himself and change pants before anyone saw him. He knew he was going to kill Bigfoot and JoJo, but he didn't want even them to see his embarrassment.

Charging through the rear door he tossed the empty machine gun on the kitchen table and began tearing at his pants to get them off. They fell to the floor and he kicked them aside. He knew he had to hurry before JoJo and Bigfoot figured another way out of the barn, but he couldn't stand the thought of having defecation all over his lower body.

He climbed into the shower and turned on the water full force. Then screamed again in rage as he stepped out and ripped off his shirt. He stepped back in and directed the showerhead to where his mess was. By this time he was panting and growling in an almost un-human manner.

"I'll kill them!" he kept muttering, "I'll kill them deader 'n hell! Screw with my plans, will they!? I'll show 'em!"

He got out of the shower and hurried to his bedroom where he grabbed some clean and dry clothing. Then he ran into the pantry where he had stashed several guns along with ammunition. He quickly re-loaded the uzi and a short-barreled .38 that he shoved into his waist- band. He was about to run out the back door when he saw through the window a car pull into his driveway. It was a police car.

Kirk aimed the uzi through the window, then lowered it. The deputy was walking slowly but purposefully toward his front door. Seeing the law officer hadn't pulled out his gun, Kirk decided to wait and see what he wanted.

He quickly buttoned his shirt, hiding the .38, propped the uzi behind the door and stepped out onto the porch.

"Hello officer," he greeted with a smile, "What brings you out this way?"

"Howdy Sir. Are you Mister Kirk?"

"Yes I am. Can I help you?"

"Mister Kirk, I'm Deputy Barney. I need to tell you to be on the lookout for some escaped convicts. A bunch of them there low-lifes done escaped from the jail, and they killed a couple of good ol' boy guards while doin' it! They're mighty dangerous Mister Kirk, and me and Sheriff Taylor is a-warnin' folks to be extra careful."

" You're Deputy Barney, and your boss is Sheriff Taylor?" Kirk asked, trying to hide a smile. "Well, that's certainly considerate and thoughtful of you, Deputy," said Kirk as he chuckled inside, "Surely you and the sheriff are going to need help in rounding up all those bad guys."

"Yessir," answered the deputy, "Sheriff Taylor has done went and called the state police so they can put out a state-wide APB."

" Well I sure hope you catch them soon so us decent folk can rest in peace." stated Kirk, "I'll definitely be keeping a sharp eye out. Do you have a card so I'll know who to call if I see anything suspicious?"

"Yessir, I shore do!" Deputy Barney said as he pulled a business card from his shirt pocket.

"Here you are, Sir. Hey, have you checked your barn lately to see if maybe someone might be in there?"

Kirk felt a moment of panic, then smiled; "Yes, I was just in the barn about ten minutes ago. I'm still trying to decide how l want to fix this old place up."

The deputy nodded, then shook Kirk's hand. "Well Sir, like I said, you be real careful.'

"I will, deputy, I surely will."

Kirk watched as the deputy walked to his car, and glanced toward the barn to see if there was anything to attract the man's attention. Bigfoot and JoJo hadn't made any noise of course; they didn't want to go back to jail. From where he stood, though, the bullet holes in the barn door looked big as Oprah Winfrey's butt, and he sure hoped the lawman didn't notice them.

With his hand behind his back near the hidden gun, Kirk watched until the deputy got in his squad car, made a gravel-spewing "u" turn and drive off.

He re-entered the house and grabbed the uzi. As near as he could figure, Bigfoot should be out of bullets now. But he wasn't taking any chances that he might have miscounted.

He crept around the far side of the barn seeking another knothole or crack he could peer through. He found nothing suitable at eye-level but did see hole about three feet above his head near the front door.

Kirk hurried back inside the house and grabbed a kitchen chair. Placing it under the hole he had observed, he climbed up quietly and peeked inside. He saw JoJo standing by the bus's open door looking confused, and heard Bigfoot trying to start the bus. The engine turned over a couple of times, then water spewed from under the hood. He could see a large puddle of oil on the ground under the bus.

Bigfoot kept trying to start the bus, but the engine simply wouldn't catch. Kirk could hear him cussing angrily, and grinned. He was about to try sticking the uzi through the hole and spraying the inside of the barn again, when he had another thought.

"Damn!" he thought to himself, "I should have thought of this in the first place." Jumping down from the chair he hurried around to the side of the barn where he knew most of the prisoners were laying in the drugged stupor. He held his mouth close to the side of the barn and began speaking loudly.

"Wake up! Wake up and obey me. You will do everything I tell you to do. You will obey my voice and only my voice. Wake up!" Running around to his original knothole, he peeked in.

He was rewarded by the sight of the men stirring around as they stood up. "Oh yes…oh yes. That's right…that's right.", Kirk whispered to himself happily. He saw Bigfoot step out of the bus and point the gun in his direction. He could plainly hear the "click" of the hammer hitting an empty chamber.

"Bigfoot, I must tell you that you and JoJo are really in a bad situation now." he yelled through the knothole.

"Let me out of here asshole, and I'll show you a bad situation!" screamed Bigfoot.

"Speaking of assholes," Kirk said with a laugh, "Kiss yours goodbye." he spoke again in his command voice: "Kill them. Kill Bigfoot and JoJo. Do it now!"

Peering through the knothole again, he saw his newly made zombies shuffling toward the other two men. JoJo screamed and tried to get into the bus but tripped and fell. He got back up and Bigfoot pushed him out of the way and jumped into the bus, shutting him out.

The zombies grabbed JoJo and began biting him, while others climbed up on the hood of the bus and broke out the windshield by hitting it repeatedly with their fists. Several of them managed to enter the bus and Kirk could hear Bigfoot yelling and cussing as he tried to fight his way out. Soon he, too, was quiet and Kirk knew it was all over.

Billy Kirk knew he was on his way now. All the people who were out to get him, and that was everybody, would be greatly surprised when he got them first. He hurried around and opened the barn door. Stepping inside he called out:

"All of you come to me. Right now." He waited impatiently as the group of former prisoners gathered in front of him. They all had a vacant stare in their eyes, and they moved slowly in a shuffling gate. But his chest swelled with pride; this was the beginning of his army.

"Bring JoJo to me." he ordered. Two of the zombies he had been speaking directly to, turned and went back inside the barn. In a moment they re-appeared with JoJo's body dragging between them.

"Now bring me Bigfoot's body."

When they had done so, Kirk brought the chair around and sat down to wait, leaning the uzi against the back of the chair. His dead army stood silently, gently swaying in their lack of coordination. He watched Bigfoot and JoJo, and soon saw a flicker of movement from each of them.

"Bigfoot, get up!" he ordered.

"JoJo, get your ass up!"

He couldn't contain his laughter. These two were also part of his army now. But he had a score to settle with them. They had tried to screw up his plans. Had almost succeeded.

"Bigfoot, take off your jump-suit." He watched with a grin as Bigfoot's clumsy fingers fumbled with the buttons that ran from his neck down to his crotch. Gradually the buttons were un-done and Bigfoot stepped out of the jail clothing. Kirk's grin grew bigger as he saw his orders being obeyed.

"JoJo, kneel in front of Bigfoot and bite off his dick." When JoJo did as he was told Kirk nearly fell out of his chair with laughter. He noticed that Bigfoot gave no sign of pain or even acknowledged what had happened to him. He stood there silently, waiting for his orders.

JoJo still knelt in place with the severed penis in his mouth. Kirk's own penis was growing rigid; his feeling of supreme power was more than just intoxicating. It was also the strongest sexual turn-on he had ever felt.

"It's going to be so great to be king of the world!" he kept thinking.

"JoJo, bite off his balls."

Kirk pointed at two of the other zombies.

"Chew off Bigfoot's ass-cheeks until there's nothing left." He told them. His insanity was reaching almost the point of over-flow. He watched and giggled and masturbated as his orders were obeyed. Drool was leaking from his mouth and his eyes were glazed as he watched and his hand worked frantically. When he climaxed, he fell off the chair in a dead faint.

Chapter Seven

As the men were milling around the tables examining the various knives and swords, Big M and Hank were also checking out each other's wares. Big M was setting aside a few weapons he was considering trading for or buying. At another table Hank was doing the same thing.

Two-foot picked up a sword and pretended he was sword fighting as he approached Black Jack.

"On guard; you swine!" Two-foot said in mock-anger, "I'll shiver yer timbers and avast yer swabs, then make you walk the plank!"

Jack just grinned half-drunkenly and reached behind his back.

"You short shit! You still taking knives to gun-fights?" and pulled out the .38. All those around the two men broke out in laughter.

Two-foot stepped back, dropped to his knees and acted terrified;

"Ohhh Massa, massa, please don't shoot me dead. I sho' nuff promise I gonna tote that barge and lift that there bale. I won't even sleep in da Big House tonight, Massa; I gonna sleep in the barn with da hosses." By now everyone had stopped what they were doing and were watching the by-play between Black Jack and Two-foot.

Black Jack stood up, put his hands on his hips and glared down at Two-foot.

"You ain't sleeping in the barn with my good horses, you dawg!" he too, started laughing and had to lean back against the wall for support.

"You gonna sleep in the cotton field tonight, Boy! And in the mornin' you'd better have a full sack o' cotton!"

Two-foot was laughing so hard he was clutching his stomach. After several seconds he reached his hand up and Jack grabbed it land pulled him to his feet. They hugged each other, still laughing. Then Jack fell back against the wall and sank into his seat, knocking over a beer bottle.

Skidmark made a mad grab for the bottle and snagged it before it hit the floor.

"Hey Dude," he said in admonishment, "You don't wanna be wasting the beer."

"Yeah," chimed in Cowboy, "There's people in this world starving to death, and here you are trying to waste the beer!" The laughter was interrupted by T.T. and Short-stuff as they quickly came through the front door.

"Sheriff's outside!" they both said in a loud whisper.

"Try to stall him a minute!" said Dandy also in a loud whisper. He hurried toward a back room where he kept the bar's linen supplies.

Jack, Two-foot, Cowboy and Skidmark stepped outside and acted like they were talking to Bow-legged Sally and Peanuts who were still sitting at the picnic table drinking their beer and eating hamburgers.

Two-foot looked over as the sheriff got out of his squad car.

"Howdy, Sheriff." he called out, "Y'all catch them escaped convicts yet?"

The lawman stopped beside them and removed his hat. Wiping the sweat from his brow, he shook his head.

"Nope. But I kind of feel they're somewhere nearby. Homer Caldwell who lives down the road about five miles was out on his front porch nearly all night, and he says no jail bus came by his place."

"How do you know he's right?" asked Two-foot, "Why would he be on his front porch all night?"

"His teenaged daughter snuck out of the house earlier, and he was sitting on the porch waiting for her to come home. He said she got in about five a.m."

"He shoulda beat her ass!" declared Black Jack, "Did he?"

"I reckon he did. I know Homer, he's a good man. But strict. I didn't ask if he did because I didn't wanna hear something I might have to arrest him for."

"You're Sheriff Taylor, right?" asked Two-foot as he stuck out his hand.

"Yes sir."

"Do you by any chance have a deputy named Barney?" Two-foot asked with a grin.

"As a matter of fact I do." answered the sheriff, "Do you know him?"

"No, I don't think so." Returned Two-foot; "I was just askin. There wouldn't happen to be an Opie and Aunt Bea in town would there?" He and Big M looked at each other and rolled their eyes.

"Why, yes actually." responded Taylor, "Uncle Opie and Aunt Bea run the new Beauty Salon and Transmission Shop across the river. They're nice folks. Let's step inside out of this heat." He continued and moved toward the door.

The three bikers moved also, making sure they were in front of him and blocking the door. They entered slowly, further blocking the door by shoving and jostling each other good naturedly while trying to give Dandy as much time as he needed.

Once inside the sheriff paused a moment to let his eyes adjust to the dimness.

"Wanna beer, sheriff?" hollered Dandy.

"No, better make it a diet Pepsi." Taylor responded, "And how about a cheeseburger with everything on it too?". He was looking around the bar at the bikers as they sat drinking or played pool. He noticed some tables shoved up against the wall with table- cloths covering whatever was on them.

"What's under the table cloths?" he asked Two-foot.

"Just some pizzas." The short biker answered, "trying to keep the bugs off of 'em till everybody else gets here and we can eat."

The sheriff nodded slowly while watching Two-foot's face. He glanced over toward the tables again.

"Well, you make sure you keep those pizzas in the right hands. Know what I mean?"

"No problem sheriff," offered Dandy, "we're keeping a sharp eye on 'em."

Sheriff Taylor took a drink of his Pepsi, then bit into his cheeseburger. As he chewed, he spoke again.

"Like I said earlier, I think those escapees are somewhere in this area. You fellas be careful while you're out ridin'. We don't know how many of them are armed, or what kind of weapons they might have."

"We'll be watchin' for 'em sheriff." said Cowboy, "but we ain't too worried; we got 'em out-numbered."

"Yeah," laughed Black Jack, "and just give Two-foot a beer bottle and he'll attack all of 'em at once!"

Taylor looked at Two-foot and nodded with a smile.

"And if that doesn't work," he said with a chuckle, "You can always hit them with a pizza, right?" The bikers all looked at him for a moment, then joined in the laughter. Taylor finished his cheeseburger and stood up to reach into his pocket.

"Forget it sheriff," said Dandy, "that's on the house."

Taylor put on his hat, picked up his Pepsi and turned toward the door.

"Guess I'll hit the road, got some bad guys to find." He said as everyone bid him farewell. He glanced once more at the covered tables, shook his head, mumbled; "Pizzas!" and smiled as he went out the door.

"Whew!" breathed Big M, "thought he was gonna bust us, there for a minute."

"I wasn't too worried," said Dandy, "he knows I run a clean place here, and he knows you guys have never caused any trouble around here. I just wanted to make sure the stuff wasn't staring him in the face."

Chapter Eight

Billy Kirk opened his eyes. He had no idea how long he had been unconscious. He stirred slowly, then sat up. The chair was still sitting upright beside him. "Musta passed out." he mumbled to himself as he got up. After restoring his flaccid penis to its home in his pants, he wiped his hand on his shirt and faced his army of zombies.

He saw Bigfoot still standing in front of him, naked. The two men he had ordered to "eat his ass" had continued their freakish dining since no one had told them to stop. There was no flesh left on Bigfoot's backside, nor on the backs of his thighs. From the bottom of his spine to the backs of his knees nothing but bone showed.

Even as he watched Bigfoot collapsed to the ground and the two men crawled atop him and continued biting and chewing.

"Enough!" Kirk growled, "Stand up."

The pair of flesh-eaters stood and faced Kirk. Bigfoot was making spastic movements with his arms and feet, but showing no signs of pain.

"Get up Bigfoot!" Kirk ordered.

Bigfoot struggled to rise, but every time he got almost to his feet, he collapsed again. There were no muscles to hold him up.

"Well that's just great!" Kirk exclaimed, "You're absolutely no use to me now, asshole." He grabbed the uzi and stood over Bigfoot's twitching form. He began firing the weapon into the fallen man's head until there was nothing left.

"JoJo, swallow that dick and help put Bigfoot's body in the bus!"

As he watched them obey him he remembered the bus was now inoperable. He smacked his palm against his forehead in exasperation.

"Shit! Shit! Shit!" he cursed as he kicked over the chair and stomped around in circles for several moments. He stopped dumbfounded, as he saw all the zombies suddenly squat and start shitting in their jumpsuits.

"What the bloody hell you idiots doing?" he screamed in frustration. "Stand up and stand still!" he ordered. Kirk stood and glared at them for several moments trying to figure out what to do next.

"I need some way to transport these idiots…I mean, my army to the battle-field." He muttered to himself.

He actually didn't know where his battlefield was going to be….just someplace with a lot of people his army could bite and transform into fellow zombies.

"Where the hell am I going to get another bus?" he asked himself, he turned to the standing dead men and almost asked them, then realized how useless that would be. He also noticed they were beginning to stink, and the ones standing directly in the sunlight were showing the effects of that sunlight. Their dead flesh was rotting and their eyeballs were swelling.

"Get back into the barn!" he ordered, "Get into the shade." He didn't really care about their well-being but he wanted to make sure they were still able to be the indestructible warriors he wanted them to be.

When they were all inside and he got close enough to close and lock the door, Kirk caught the strong whiff of multiple loads of defecation. He bent over and puked. He stood, wiped his mouth and then went inside his house and poured himself a glass of wine. He sat down at the kitchen table and began trying to figure out where he could get another bus, or some other vehicle large enough to haul around his eighteen-man army.

Finishing his drink he left and got in his black Blazer. He began driving slowly in the direction of town, carefully eyeing both sides of the road. Not really sure what he was looking for, he kept scanning the nearby countryside for something of a vehicular nature that might serve his purpose.

As he was navigating a gentle curve in the two-lane road he saw a day-care center on his left. Almost past it, he noticed a small shuttle bus that had been converted for the day care's use. He pulled into the parking lot and sat looking at the bus for several minutes.

It wasn't as large as the jail transport bus his escapees had used, but maybe if he had them sitting in each other's laps they could all be crammed into the bus. They certainly wouldn't notice any discomfort and, frankly, he couldn't have cared less if they did.

As he watched he saw a small fenced-in playground on one side of the center. He began to visualize an army of zombie children. They didn't have to big and tough, they only had to bite people, and hell; any kid can do that.

Kirk chuckled at the thought and of how easy it would be for the children to approach adults. In fact most grow-ups would probably try to pick up any wandering child they might see, and that would give the kid the opportunity to bite them and there-by draft them into his army.

He considered returning to the farm and bringing five or six of the zombies back here so they could take over the day care center and infect the kids and whatever adult workers there might be. Having nearly made that decision, Kirk was slowly backing up in the parking lot when two other cars pulled in at practically the same time.

The cars parked and the mothers got out and entered the day care in order to retrieve their children. It was late afternoon and he knew more parents would be arriving on an irregular basis. The risk of him being stopped, or worse; captured made him change his plans.

Cussing in frustration, he laid about six feet of burnt rubber as he peeled out of the parking lot and continued on down the highway. Narrowly missing a pick-up truck pulling a wagonload of hay bales, he screamed profanities at the driver, flipped him off, and speeded up.

Traffic was increasing as the local folks were getting off work and heading home.

"These damned dumb hillbillies need to get out of my way!" he muttered to himself angrily. When he realized how fast he was going, Kirk made himself slow down so as not to attract attention, and began driving up and down various side streets of town, hoping to see a vehicle he could use.

He drove around for another hour or so to no avail. Trying to decide which way to go at a particular intersection, he realized he was hungry. He made a "u" turn and headed back in the direction of the Hog Jowl Inn, figuring he could something to eat, though it wouldn't be anything to write home about, and maybe some information as well.

A few minutes later he pulled into the parking lot, which was already beginning to fill up. He hurried inside hoping to get a table by himself. He was in luck and seated himself at the last two-chair table left.

In a couple of minutes a heavily rouged and mascara'd waitress approached. It was Hannah, the waitress who had waited on him at his first visit when he met Officer Jemson. He put forth his best friendly persona.

"Hello Hannah, how are you this fine day?"

"Ohh, hello mister Kirk. I'm fine. What can I get you? The meatloaf is our specialty today."

"No, I think I'll have the chicken-fried steak. You folks make it so well." He answered with a fake smile, all the while thinking: *"Well enough to puke a buzzard off a gut-wagon!"*

'Has Officer Jemson been in today?"

Hannah gasped, bringing one hand to her mouth in dismay.

"Oh mister Kirk, haven't you heard? LeRoy was killed sometime night-before last. Some guys escaped from jail and shot him and another guard named Roscoe Havens."

"Oh no! Are you serious?" Kirk pretended shock and disbelief.

"Are there any clues? Where did they go?"

Hannah just shook her head sadly, "No one knows where they are, but Sheriff Taylor thinks they may still be in the area some place."

"Hannah," said Kirk with an air of gentle seriousness; "If there is anything I can do, be sure to let me know."

"Thank you, mister Kirk. I will. Hey, I'd better get your supper before you starve to death." She said forcing a smile as she hurried back toward the kitchen. He found it difficult to keep his eyes off her delicious backside as she walked away.

Billy Kirk chuckled to himself as he thought about how dumb these country hicks were. Although with Taylor thinking the escapees may still be near-by could be a problem. He needed the sheriff and all the other cops to concentrate their search further out so he and his army could move about a little more freely.

He had finished his meal left a three-dollar tip on the table and was standing in line at the register waiting to pay when the sheriff entered. Taylor was in the line waiting to pick up his carryout order when Kirk paid his bill and walked over to him.

"Good evening Sheriff." Kirk said as he offered his hand, "I'm Billy Kirk. Just bought a place right out of town recently."

The sheriff shook his hand and nodded. "Pleased to meet you, mister Kirk. I heard you had bought the old Cartwright place. Hope you're getting settled in alright."

"Yes Sir, I am. I got a great deal on the place, a real bonanza you might say. I'm still trying to decide what all I want to do with it though.", Kirk answered, "Hey you know," he continued, "I was talking to Hannah and she said you seem to think those escaped convicts might still be in the area. Is that right?"

"Yeah, I kind of do. I don't think there's any cause for you to be alarmed, Mister Kirk, just be careful and keep a sharp eye out. And if you see anything or anyone suspicious, call it in quick."

"Oh, I will.", Kirk agreed, "But I was just thinking. If I was one of those guys I would want to get as far from here as possible. Because, for one thing; you'd be looking for me, and also because probably most of the local people would recognize me if I showed my face."

"So, you'd want to be far enough away so that no one would recognize you, is that right?" added the officer.

"Yes Sir, I think I would.", said Kirk seriously, "But that's just my thoughts. I'm sure you know more about it than I do."

Taylor paid for his order and picked it up.

"Thanks for your thoughts, Mister Kirk. I'll keep that in mind."

"No problem Sheriff, anything I can do to help." responded Kirk and walked out the door. Taylor watched him thoughtfully for a moment, then got in his county car and drove off.

Kirk was about to start his own car when he noticed the shuttle bus from the day care center pull into the lot. He sat still and watched as nice-looking middle-aged woman got out and went into the restaurant. He watched her as she walked away from him. Her tight skirt showed the shape of her butt very well, and she seemed to be very well built in the chest department too, he thought. *Do all these country women have such nice-shaped asses!?* He wondered to himself.

She had left the motor running, so Kirk knew she wouldn't be inside very long.

"*Now that's what I call Fate,*" he grinned to himself, "*my transportation solution dropped right into my hands.*"

He quickly got out of his car and walked casually over to the shuttle bus. Looking around to make sure no one was looking in his direction, he opened a side door and crawled in, shutting the door behind him. He scooted up as close as possible to the back of the front seats and lay still on the floor. He waited.

Soon, he heard the sound of approaching footsteps on the gravel. He tried not to breathe as he felt the door open and the woman climb inside. Shutting the door she put the gearshift in Drive and was slowly pulling out of the parking lot.

Sensing they were on the main road, Kirk raised up behind the woman and wrapped his arm around her neck. It was still light outside, so Kirk kept his head turned away from the window so no passing cars could see his face if they happened to be looking in that direction.

"Just do what I tell you, and you'll be okay. Understand?" he whispered hoarsely in her ear.

"Yesss,", she managed to gasp, "Please don't hurt me…I can't breathe…."

Kirk relaxed his hold a little and she began taking deep breaths.

"Where are you going?", he asked her.

"Home, I'm going home. I'll do anything, just please don't hurt me." she pleaded.

"Don't worry. I just want this bus.", Kirk assured her,

"You live at the day care center?"

If she was surprised by his knowledge of where she worked, she showed no sign of it, figuring he had probably read the information on the side of the bus. "Yes, in the back."

"Where's your husband?" he asked her.

"I'm not…I mean he'll be home soon too." She said quickly. She gasped again as his arm tightened on her throat.

"Don't lie to me, bitch." He growled in her ear, "When we get there if I see anyone else I'll kill them. Then I'll kill you. Do you understand me?"

She struggled to answer; "Yessss" came out in a hoarse whisper. As his arm relaxed again, she continued; "There's no one there. I promise."

"There now, that's better." Kirk whispered softly, "See how easy that was?"

Kirk glanced out the front windshield and could see they were nearing the day care center.

"Just pull into the parking lot like you always do.", he ordered.

"Turn it off and give me the keys." She did so.

"Now lay down on the seat and hide your eyes.", he told her.

As she leaned over to comply, Kirk's hand brushed against her full breast and he felt a tingle in his groin.

He got out and quickly opened the front door. She lay sideways on the seat with her face covered. Her skirt had ridden up her thigh and he could see the bottom edge of her panty leg. Her legs looked smooth and warm. He groaned inside, knowing he was going to have to have her, but not knowing if he had time.

He ran his hand from her knee up her thigh to her hip. "Please don't…", she said in a muffled voice. Kirk was so aroused now he didn't care if there was time or not, he was going to have her.

He grabbed her by the hair and pulled her out of the vehicle.

"Take me into the house.", he ordered the frightened woman. Handing her purse to her, he used his other hand to jab his finger into her back.

"I don't want to shoot you, but I will if you give me any trouble. Understand?", he poked the finger into her back even harder, pretending it was his gun.

"You…you said you just wanted the bus." She protested nervously.

"I do." Kirk agreed. "That's all I wanted until I saw up your skirt. It's been weeks since I've had any sex. And I sure need some.", his voice was getting hoarse and his throat was dry. As soon as they entered the house he kicked shut the door behind him.

"Where's the bedroom!?", he panted. The woman began weeping softly as she led him toward the back of the house. As they neared the bed Kirk still stood behind her with his finger in her back.

"Reach over there and pull the slip off that pillow." he told her. When she had obeyed, he had her put it over her head, covering her face.

"Now," he whispered with a ragged sigh, "we can relax and take it easy. Take off everything except your panties."

She whimpered as she began removing her clothing. He watched her silently as he unbuckled his belt and lowered his pants. His erection was so hard it was painful.

He ran his hands over her nude body, fondling her heavy breasts and jiggling them in his palms.

"Very nice…" he whispered to himself. Suckling one of her breasts, he shoved his left hand down the front of her panties and his right hand down the back. He let his fingers explore her womanhood freely. She whimpered again.

"Listen to me," he panted in her ear after letting her breast drop from his mouth, "Just do what I tell you to do and you'll be alright. It'll all be over in a few minutes. I won't hurt you. Besides, you'll probably like it once I slip it in you.", he chuckled as a thought entered his mind; "If you knew who I am you'd be proud to let me do you. I'm famous, lady, and I've laid some of the finest women in Hollywood. You're lucky I think you're sexy." Pinching her butt, he giggled.

Kirk pulled his hands out of her underwear and put them on her shoulders, pushing her back onto the bed. As she lay back he yanked her panties off, stepped between her legs and entered her violently.

The woman turned her head away and sobbed as he ravaged her.

Billy Kirk pulled up his pants breathing heavily, a look of satisfaction on his face.

"Roll over on your stomach." He ordered. She obeyed with a soft whimper.

"Put your hands behind your back." When she had done so, Kirk snatched one of her stockings off the floor and tied her hands together.

Standing between her legs, he looked down at her butt. He ran his hands lovingly over her buttocks; kneading them and squeezing them admiringly.

"Damn!" he exclaimed, "Do all you country girls have such nice asses?" He bent over and kissed each butt cheek, then stood again.

"I wish I had more time Honey. But in a few hours I'll be in control of this town and I promise I'll be back to get you."

He hurried out the door, entered the shuttle bus and took off. He briefly wondered about his Blazer back at the diner's parking lot, then realized he needn't worry because in a few hours he would control everything around here and wouldn't have to worry about the police or anything else.

Not wanting to attract attention, he stayed within the speed limit, though it was difficult. He had a world to conquer and this was wasting time. He passed a bar on his left that had a bunch of motorcycles parked in front.

"Bunch of society's misfits!" he said to himself as he went by. Then he started laughing to himself.

"They'll make the perfect addition to my army. My troops should be able to take them down without any problem. They won't know what hit them." He was still laughing when he pulled into his driveway and eased back to the barn.

Billy opened the barn doors in order to drive the shuttle bus inside out of sight. However, the jail transport bus was parked in the way. He got out of the vehicle and called his "army" over.

"Push that bus further into the barn out of the way." he ordered. He smiled in satisfaction as the former-men began pushing the bus. Even with all of them pushing they were barely making any headway. The bus' wheels skidded slowly over the ground.

"Take it out of gear you dammed idiots!" screamed Kirk. He stormed past the laboring zombies and entered the bus. Angrily he jerked the transmission into neutral, and was nearly thrown off his feet as the bus suddenly lurched forward.

He jumped up into the seat and let it roll forward several feet until it was nearly at the other end of the barn, then he slammed on the breaks and put it in gear again. The sudden stop caused Bigfoot's dead body to slide down the aisle, and Kirk nearly tripped over it as he got out of the bus.

"Okay, you can stop now." he said as he walked back to the smaller vehicle. The orange-suited felons were milling around in confusion, waiting for orders.

"Stand at attention until I return." he ordered them. He walked past the small bus and into the farmhouse where he went to the bathroom to relieve his bladder. On the way back out again, he paused long enough to pick up the uzi which had been laying on the table.

"Move away from the door." he demanded as he was about to get in the driver's seat. His attention was captured by the sound of another vehicle and he turned toward the driveway in time to see the sheriff's squad car pulling in.

Knowing the lawman had seen the shuttle bus and the orange-suited men, Kirk felt he had no choice. He raised the uzi and began firing at the officer. He emptied the clip and was about to run into the house for another one when the car rapidly reversed and spun out of the driveway spewing twin rooster-tails of gravel in his direction.

Kirk was almost in a panic now. He knew the sheriff would have reinforcements in a matter of minutes. He had to get his army down to that stupid biker bar so they could "draft" them into his service.

"You guys hurry up and get into the bus. Now!" he shouted as he hurried toward the house for more ammunition.

Chapter Nine

Black Jack watched with a smile as the boys gathered around the tables again and began comparing weapons. His arm was around T.T. and he said to Two-foot: "Why aren't you over there checkin' out all the swords?"

Two-foot looked at him and grinned, "Hell, Bro; I got enough knives already. Besides, Partner doesn't trust me around sharp instruments." Both men laughed.

"Are you gonna check 'em out Honey?" asked T.T. as she snuggled up to him and handed him his beer.

"Nope," he answered, taking a long drink of the cold amber liquid, "long as I got my .38, I'm ready for anything."

T.T. leaned forward and let the tip of her tongue tickle his ear. "You ready for me, Baby?" she asked with a flirty whisper.

Black Jack let out a short, deep laugh, "I'm always ready for you Sweet-cakes." Bringing his big hand up, he knuckled one of her small nipples and was pleased to see it harden under her tank top. He saw Two-foot nearby throwing his knife at the dartboard.

"Hey Two-foot," he said, "Make sure none of these butt-heads drink my beer while I'm gone." Two-foot grinned and nodded, wishing he had his lady with him. His wife, Partner, had to stay home and take care of a couple of grandkids today, and couldn't make the ride. He shook his head wistfully as he watched Jack take T.T. into the women's bathroom.

Two-foot looked around the bar room at the bikers and their women. Most of the men were still gathered around the display of weapons Big M and Hank had spread out. A few were shooting pool, and some were just sitting at the bar or at tables drinking and talking.

"*These guys are my family.*" He thought proudly, "*These are the best people in the world!*" He felt himself getting emotional, which he usually did when he'd been drinking. After several beers he would either get maudlin and reflective about his life, or want to pick a fight. Unfortunately, he didn't win all the fights he got into, and as he had aged he realized he didn't heal up nearly as fast as he used to. He grunted and tried to snap out of it.

"Hey Skidmark," he called across the room, "I guess you won the race by default. Big M didn't show up for it."

"Yep," laughed Skidmark, "De-fault was his, not mine. He's too busy trying work some deals over there." He came over to Two-foot and picked up some darts.

"Probably just as well," he continued, "he couldn't have won anyway." Throwing a dart, he grimaced as it missed the board and stuck in the wall. "It'll be dark pretty soon anyway," he burped loudly, "Ain't no time to be speeding around all those curves and switch-backs."

"Yeah, no shit." said Two-foot; "Too many deer out there just waiting to cross right in front of you." He burped too, trying to make it louder than Skidmark's had been.

Short-stuff came over and started to go toward the women's bathroom. Two-foot touched her arm, "Can you wait a few minutes? Jack and T.T. are in there." He grinned.

"No, I can't wait. My bladder's about to bust." she answered doing a little dance. Two-foot put his arm around her shoulder and led her toward the men's room.

"You go ahead on in there. I'll make sure no one comes in.", he said, noticing that he was starting to slur his words.

"Thanks Hon." She said as she hurried in and closed the door. Two-foot placed himself in front of the door with his feet spread and his arms across his chest. He was now on official guard-duty and nobody was gonna get past him come hell or high water or democrats.

Skidmark threw another dart, missed again, and took another drink. He glanced at Two-foot, shrugged and grinned.

"You desertin' me for guard duty?" he asked with a fake whine.

"Hey Skid," Two-foot answered, "You were one of them there marines, you know how important guard duty is."

Skidmark gave out a long, loud belch and nodded his head. " Sir, Yes Sir," he said loudly with an almost perfect salute, "I remember those days. At least; some of them." he stood still, wavering a little bit and remembering. "That, my brother, was a whole different world."

Two-foot nodded his agreement.

"I know, Bro." He said seriously, "I tried my damndest to enlist, but the warden just wouldn't let me out."

Skidmark walked over to Two-foot and gave him a big hug, "I know, man, you told me. You said he told you that the very thought of turning you loose with a gun was totally bizarre." he said sympathetically. "You should been there with us, we'd had a ball."

Short-stuff came out of the bathroom. She and Two-foot high-fived each other and she said: Thanks. I'll do the same for you some time."

"No prob.", Two-foot said, then burped. Skidmark followed suit with his own burp.

"You two bad-assed bikers havin' a burpin' contest?" she asked with a laugh.

Two-foot got a serious, strained look on his face, then let out a loud, long burp. Then he looked at Skidmark and smiled.

"Beat that, Homey." He said.

Skidmark shook his head and declared; "Homey don't play that shit." Then bent over and farted toward Two-foot.

"Ahh hell, that ain't fair!" laughed Short-stuff, "I'm leavin'!", she made her way back over to where Big M and Hank were sitting at a table just in time to hear Hank ask Big M:

"Hey, do you know why you can never solve a Redneck murder?'

"No," groaned Big M, "But I think you're gonna tell me. Right?"

"Right! It's because all the DNA is the same, and there are no dental records!" He laughed loudly at his own joke while Big M and Short-stuff just looked at him sadly.

Short-stuff nudged Big M's shoulder and nodded back toward Two-foot and Skidmark.

"Damn! Skid," They could hear Two-foot exclaim as he backed away from the other man, "It smells like something done crawled up inside of you and died."

Black Jack and T.T. came out of the women's restroom; both were smiling.

"I kept your beer safe, big man." Two-foot said as he nodded toward the beer sitting on the table.

"Cool, Bro." answered Jack, "I'm gonna finish it, then me and the ol' lady's gonna hit the road. Gonna be getting' dark before too long."

"Yeah, I suppose I oughta be headin' out too. Partner's gonna be pissed at me stayin' out all day.", said Two-foot as he took another drink. "Besides, I wanna play around with them grandkids too."

"Well you be careful, Bro. You been downin' a lot of beer ya know."

Before Two-foot could respond, Betty Boop hollered from the door;

"Hey, everybody. Come check this out! Hurry!"

Within a few seconds practically all the bikers were crowding around the door and peering out. They saw the sheriff's squad car rolling slowly into the parking lot and smashing into the large dumpster sitting off to one side. The windshield was shattered and there were obvious bullet holes in the car's side panel.

As the car came to a rest Two-foot and Jack, along with Big M and Skidmark were running toward it. They saw sheriff Taylor slumped against the steering wheel covered in blood. Black Jack yanked the door open and Two-foot was trying to get Taylor out of the vehicle.

"What the hell happened, man?" grunted Two-foot as he struggled with the man. Skidmark reached in and helped pull the sheriff out of the car, then helped support him as they carried him into the bar.

The other men quickly pushed a couple of tables together and the sheriff was laid on them gently. He was barely conscious and in obvious pain.

"Sheriff, what happened?" asked Dandy as he was unbuttoning the hurt man's shirt. Short-stuff and Peanuts pushed their way in and took over trying to tend to him.

"That new guy…the one that bought the old Cartwright place..", gasped Taylor as he tried to explain, "raped Mrs. Cleaver over at the day care center…" he paused to catch his breath, "Then he stole their little shuttle bus. " He groaned in pain as Short-Stuff lifted him enough to see that at least one bullet had passed all the way through his right shoulder.

"Cleaver?" questioned Two-foot, "Is that June Cleaver?"

"No, it's her sister April. You know June?" asked Sandy.

"Uh, no. Just askin." said Two-foot trying to hide a grin. "*I'm either really drunk, or in the Twilight Zone.*" he thought to himself.

"I sent her to the hospital with Barney, then I…I went out to the Cartwright place to arrest the bastard…" again he had to pause long enough to catch his labored breath, "When I pulled into his driveway I saw…saw some of the escapees in their orange jump-suits standin' around. Kirk, that's the fella's name, started shootin' at me with an uzi…Blew out my radio and shot me all to hell before I could get out of there…"

"Who you want us to call, man?" asked Two-foot as he pulled out his cell phone.

Short-stuff had opened the man's shirt by now, and was trying to wipe the blood away so she could assess the wounds: two holes in his left shoulder and one in his lower right chest.

"I know these probably hurt like hell," she said to him, "but they're not life-threatening if we can stop the bleeding."

"Call the state police," Taylor managed to groan, "number's on a clip-board hangin' on my dash."

"I'll go get it." stated Cowboy and hurried out.

Everybody was gathered around the tables watching Short-stuff and Peanuts taking care of the sheriff when Cowboy came running back in.

"Hey everybody," his voice was practically a scream, "That dude's here! That shuttle bus just pulled into the parking lot!" Before he had even finished speaking nearly everyone had run to the door.

"Shit!", said Black Jack, "It's those jail-birds! They're getting off the bus."

Skidmark grabbed Two-foot by the shoulder and pulled him over so he could see out the door too. "You said you wanted a fight Bro, looks like we're gonna have a good one!"

They could see the orange-suited men moving toward them in a slow, awkward fashion. The bus driver was standing in the bus' doorway with an uzi.

"Look," said Two-foot, "the driver seems to be the only one with a weapon. If we can take him out we can kick some jail-bird ass."

"Here…here…" Taylor was moaning, and holding his firearm up, "take this and shoot that bastard! He's probably the one that broke them out of jail."

"You sure about shootin' him?" asked Big M.

"Damn right…you've got my authority to defend yourselves."

"Ahh hell, this is a dream come true., Big M grinned as he took the gun and made his way out the door.

"For me too, Bro.", laughed Black Jack, "I get to shoot a bunch of white boys and get away with it!".

"Just make sure you shoot the right one, Bro!, said Two-foot, then he pointed, "Look, there's a couple of black ones. I'll go stab their asses just to even things out a little," Jack laughed and pushed his way out the door beside Two-foot.

"Yeah, go stab 'em Two-foot. Wouldn't want anyone to think we're racists, would we?"

As they came outside the bar, Kirk saw them and raised the uzi in their direction. Black Jack and Big M both started firing at him and he fell back inside the bus without having the chance to shoot back. As the two bikers' bullets whizzed around him Billy Kirk jerked the tranny into gear and sped out of the parking lot.

A bullet had torn off part of his right ear and the blood was flowing. He couldn't believe they were actually shooting back at him. They weren't supposed to have guns, were they? He knew he had to get away and hide until his soldiers and taken over the bikers and turned them into part of his army.

He cursed loudly and hit his fist against the steering wheel. "Of course they had guns," he yelled to himself, "They're social misfits, law-breakers! Assholes!" he screamed over and over; "Assholes!" and floored the gas pedal until he saw a dirt road on his right, He turned down it in a huge cloud of dust and kept going.

Black Jack fired at and hit two other of the escapees, and started cussing when he saw the bullets had no effect on them. He shot one of them again, and again.

"Damn!" he growled; "They're like those dammed birthday candles that won't go out!"

Big M turned the gun on one of the approaching escapees and fired again. The bullet hit the man in the chest causing him to stagger backwards, but then he continued forward right toward M.

"Damn, M," said Skidmark, "you missed a target that close?"

"I didn't miss that bastard. I hit him dead center, and he's still comin'! He's not even bleedin'"

Betty-Boop and Peanuts were backed against the wall screaming as three of the orange-clad men came at them.

"What the hell is it with these guys!?", yelled Two-foot as he jumped up and planted both his booted feet in a blank face that didn't even register being kicked. "I've done kicked this dirt-wad three times and he wont' stop!"

"They're zombies!" screamed Peanuts, "They're real zombies!" she scrambled to the side and crawled under the picnic table.

"Ain't no dammed such thing as zombies!" called Cowboy as he tripped one of the attackers.

"You know that, and I know that," hollered Short-stuff, "but they don't seem to know it! Look at 'em. They've been shot and they don't bleed. Look at the way they move!" she too, was ducking out of the way.

"What ever the hell they are,", yelled Two-foot, "they smell like shit!"

One of the zombies was reaching for Short-stuff when Jynx stepped up and smashed his fist into the side of the un-human's face. Seeing it had no apparent effect, Jynx hit him again, and again. Short-stuff had scrambled out of the way and the zombie turned toward Jynx.

As the biker tried to back-pedal away he found himself against the wall. The zombie grabbed him and was biting him on the neck as Jynx screamed and struggled in the beast's stronger grip.

Short-stuff and Peanuts scurried from under the picnic table and each of them grabbed one of the zombie's arms. Jynx managed to push himself away before he collapsed, blood pouring from the open wound on his neck. The two women hurried back under the table as the zombie man dislodged them and turned toward them.

Hank and Dandy came through the door with their arms loaded with swords and knives.

"Here, use these." Ordered Dandy, "You have to cut off their heads to kill 'em"

"How the hell you know something like that?" asked Black Jack as his fist smashed into the face of an attacker. The man went down, then slowly got back up.

"I watch a lot of television." admitted Dandy defensively.

"Man, shit! This ain't funny!" asserted Black Jack as he backed away from the man.

With Big M on one end and Skidmark and Two-foot on the other end, they picked up the picnic table and charged the two nearest of the zombies; knocking them down and then dropping the table on top of them.

The sheriff's gun was empty so Big M shoved it into his belt and hurried over to Hank. Skidmark and Two-foot were already there and grabbing weapons.

"Here Bro," said M as he tossed a sword to Two-foot, "this one is longer so you don't have to get so close."

"Sounds good to me," panted Two-foot as he snatched the sword out of the air and turned toward the enemy.

"Whatever you guys do, don't let them bite you!" shouted Dandy, "If they bite you you'll turn into one of them!" he added loudly.

"More television wisdom?" asked Two-foot as he plunged his weapon into the throat of one of the walking dead men. When the man didn't fall down, but continued coming for him, Two-foot backed up a bit and muttered to himself; "If there weren't so many people around, I'd piss all over myself. This shit ain't funny at all!"

He took a mighty swing and actually chopped off the man's arm. As he jerked the blade out of the guy's chest where it had buried itself when the arm fell to the ground, he moved to the side. His target didn't even seem to notice his missing arm. He turned and lumbered toward Two-foot.

"Two-foot, look out!" he heard someone scream. Sensing a presence behind him, he ducked as another orange-suit tripped over him and fell into the one-armed man.

"Hey doctor Kimble, I've got your one-armed man." He chuckled to himself and scrambled to his feet in time to see Black Jack's sword take off the head of the man he had already shot. The dead man fell down, twitched and jerked a couple of times, then lay still.

"Shit! It works!" Jack crowed loudly, "Chop their freakin' heads off!"

Two-foot heard screaming and glanced toward the picnic table where two of the women had hidden under. A zombie was trying to reach them, and Jynx was collapsed on the ground. Two-foot hurried over, jumped up on the table and took a hefty swing that separated the zombie's head with hardly any "drag" at all as it sliced through the dead flesh.

"Man, oh man," he smiled, "This baby cuts better'n a barb wire jock strap!"

All the bikers were now armed with swords from Big M and Hank's collections, and they attacked as one; chopping and hacking their way into and through the scattered gang of zombies. Two-foot grinned, "Hell, that's way more like it!" and chopped off the man's other arm. He danced around the man chopping here and there and watching pieces of meat fly off the zombie man's body.

The escapee had no arms, or ears; his orange jump suit was in rags, and most of his stomach and shoulders were now lying on the ground, and he still kept coming.

"Okay tough guy," grunted Two-foot, "Play time is over." And with that he jumped up and swung his sword in a vicious swipe that removed the head from the shoulders it had known all its life. The head bounced and rolled away, and the body fell down.

"Now that's what I like to see." Two-foot said as he was catching his breath, "A man that knows his limitations."

He swung around to see who was next.

"Hey Two-foot," Skidmark yelled, "You just chop off their feet, that way you can reach your target."
He gave a desperate laugh as he swung at one of the orange-suited men and missed.

"Screw you very much, Brother." panted Two-foot, then jumped aside as one of the zombies tried to grab him in a bear hug.

Stumbling off balance, he was unable to avoid the cold dead hand that grabbed his vest and was pulling him closer. He was trying to bring his sword around when Cowboy stepped up and chopped off the hand. Two-foot fell away from the zombie.

"Thanks Cowboy, I owe ya one." he said as he swung his sword at the man's neck. He hit the head instead and the blade sliced into the skull and stuck. He was trying to jerk it free while at the same time trying to keep out of reach of the other hand.

"I told ya to aim for the feet, shorty." declared Skidmark as he swung again and neatly sliced off the orange-suit's head.

Mean time Two-foot was chasing after his opponent's head so he could retrieve his sword.

Looking quickly around Two-foot saw that Big M had one of them pinned to the wall while Baby Hoss chopped at the head. Baby Hoss' second swing took the head off and he had to dance out of the way to keep it from hitting him.

"Hey Bro, look at Jynx!" Two-foot heard Skidmark yell. When he looked over he saw that Jynx had gotten to his feet, but now had the same vacant look on his face, and was moving awkwardly and clumsily just like the zombies.

'That zombie bit him!" shrieked Short-stuff as Two-foot approached cautiously.

Jynx turned slowly toward Two-foot and began moving toward him.

"Jynx!" yelled Two-foot, "Jynx, wake up man. Snap out of it!"

The now-dead biker kept coming and Two-foot was slowly retreating.

"You gotta kill him Two-foot!" yelled Dandy, "He's one of them now. You gotta kill him."

"No, man. I can't…" Two-foot kept backing away from the approaching changeling. He saw Dandy run over, grab Jynx by the hair from behind, jerk his head back and slice his throat. He sliced again then stepped back as the body fell and he held the head in his hand.

"I had to, Two-foot, I had to." Dandy kept saying. He dropped the severed head, bent over and puked, utterly sickened at the horror of what he had done.

The short biker turned away so he wouldn't start puking too, and saw Cowboy hacking futilely at one of the zombies trying to grab him. Skidmark ran to the rescue faster than an illegal alien running from Immigration authorities. He chopped one of the zombie's legs off and when the undead beast fell, Skidmark told Cowboy; "Chop his dammed head off, Bro. That's what ya gotta do!"

Black Jack was standing over a fallen escapee chopping and chopping at the headless body.

"You scary freakin' bastards!" he kept yelling, "You ain't even real! What the hell you doin' scarin' the shit outta me like this!?" He stepped back, sweat pouring down his face. His eyes were big and he kept spinning around so he could see in every direction, his sword poised for striking.

"There ain't no dammed such a thing as zombies!" he yelled. T.T. ran up to him and hugged him.

"It's okay, honey. It's okay. They're all dead."

"Shit! They were already dead!" he exclaimed tiredly, "How the hell could they be moving around like that?"

"Beats the crap outta me, Bro." answered Big M. "Something sure is strange around here."

"Speakin' of shit," interrupted Two-foot, "did you notice how all them freaks smell like shit? And they've all got brown stains on the back sides of their jumpsuits."

"Hell, maybe that's what happens when you turn into a zombie." offered Cowboy. "Hey," exclaimed Two-foot, "if someone turned me into a zombie, it'd scare the shit outta me!"

"Yeah, me too." Said Skidmark. Then he continued;

"That Kirk guy was an actor," maybe they're makin' some kind of movie."

"Well if they are," declared Two-foot, "They need to get some more actors. These guys sorta lost their heads! Maybe they read the wrong script."

"I know one thing," said Black Jack as he shuddered, "Nothing like a bunch of dammed zombies to sober a man up!"

They all tried to laugh but couldn't quite pull it off. "Yeah, no shit!" said Two-foot, "I think I need a drink."

"Jynx is really dead, isn't he?" questioned Short-stuff.

"Yeah Honey,", said Big M, "I saw what happened. Dandy had to do it, or Jynx mighta bit more of us."

Just then Short-stuff screamed and pointed. They turned and saw Betty Boop lying on the ground by the sheriff's car and one of the zombies leaning over her.

Big M and Two-foot ran over and Two-foot began hacking at the undead' thing's leg while Big M was trying to reach its head. His sword kept digging into the beast's shoulders and back, having little effect.

Two-foot managed to chop off one of the zombie's arms as it continued trying to reach the unconscious Betty Boop. Just then Skidmark arrived and grabbed the orange-suit from behind, jerking it upright where Big M's sword quickly separated its head from its body. The head bounced off the sheriff's car and rolled onto the ground.

Short-stuff hurried over as Skidmark shoved the headless body aside where it fell against the dumpster and dropped to the ground.

"Is she alright? Did he bite her?"

"I don't know, Babe, we gotta watch her for a minute to see." Replied Big M.

"Maybe we oughta tie her hands behind her." Suggested Two-foot.

Yeah," agreed Black Jack hurrying up. "At least long enough to see if she's been turned into one of them Things."

Just then Betty stirred, opened her eyes widely and screamed. Her head swung back and forth wildly;

"Did you get him?" she asked frantically. "Did you get him?"

Short-stuff bent over and helped her up, putting her arm around her.

"Dammed right we got him, Sister." She said as she was leading the shaken, frightened woman toward the bar door.

"How many of them are there?" Asked Big M.

Black Jack and Two-foot began a quick count of the orange-suited bodies lying about.

"I counted eighteen." Said Two-foot.

"That's what I got too." Agreed Jack.

"Hell," exclaimed Big M, "The sheriff said there were nineteen escapees. There's another one around here someplace."

"We'd better search the place." Stated Two-foot.

"Look, it's the sheriff." said Jack nodding toward the door. Sheriff Taylor was standing in the doorway leaning against the frame trying to hold himself up.

"I could hear what was going on," he said quietly, "Help me over so I can see."

As Big M and Black Jack put their arms around him and half-carried him over to one of the bodies, Jack called to Cowboy;

"One of them freaks is missing. You guys look around and find him. But be careful!" The sheriff bent down to look at the severed head.

"Yep, that's JoJo Carter alright. He was standing trial for rape. I'm not a coroner or nothing like that, but from the lack of blood I'd guess he's been dead several hours."

He pointed to another head that lay facing them.

"I think his name was Bobby Blake. Shot his wife with a berretta pistol."

The two bikers helped him over to another head that seemed to be just lying around doing nothing.

"That's Mike L. Jackson…a child abuser." He was shaking his head in confusion, as he had them help him back inside. Seated at a table holding a bar towel to the wound in his stomach, he told

Black Jack; "Call everybody inside." Black Jack started for the door but Short-stuff and Peanuts were already calling for everyone.

As the other BROK members entered the bar, Cowboy reported:

"Man, we looked all over the place. Didn't see any more orange suits anywhere."

"Well, everyone stay on the alert." Ordered Jack.

In a few seconds everyone was gathered around the sheriff. Sandy ran over and unplugged the jukebox so it was quiet enough to hear what the lawman was going to say.

"I don't have any idea what the deal is with those escapees, fellas. I truly don't. I don't believe in ghosts, vampires, or zombies, but they dammed sure acted like zombies, didn't they?"

Several of the bikers nodded their agreement. The sheriff continued;

"I know Kirk was involved some way. He probably broke them out, maybe he killed the two guards, I don't know. And I sure as hell don't know how he managed to turn those guys into zombies. If that's what they are. But I do know he raped the Cleaver woman, and he's sure as hell gonna pay for that!" he paused to catch his breath.

"Look fellas," he went on, "we all know no one is going to believe what went on here today. And being bikers, you guys are going to be targeted by the state police as the real bad guys."

Again the bikers nodded in agreement.

“We know, sheriff, it’s the same old shit.” said Two-foot.

“But you’re on our side, man,” stated Big M, “you know what happened.”

“Yes, I do. But I’m one man. I suggest you all hop on your bikes and head for home. Forget this ever happened. Dandy and I will figure something out.”

A few of the bikers wanted to argue about it, saying they would stay and help him do whatever was necessary, but Black Jack got their attention.

“The man’s right. We need to get our asses outta here, and right now. Surely the police are on the way by now.” He turned and shook Taylor’s hand.

“I see one of your men got it too.” said Taylor, “Leave him here. We’ll take care of him. I’ll personally notify you when you can arrange for his funeral.”

“Thanks, man. You’re okay for a cop.” He said with a grin.

They filed out and fired up their bikes. Two-foot pulled up near Big M.

“Bro, I saw which way that Kirk dude went. Wanna see if we can find him?”

Big M glanced over at Short-stuff questioningly. She shrugged and nodded.

“Just keep your big ass outta trouble.” she admonished, “I’m following Maggie home.”

“Okay, Baby.”, M said, “It’s getting’ dark, so be careful.” He turned back to Two-foot.

"I'm your huckleberry. I wanna make him pay for what happened to Jynx."

"No way, Jose," said Skidmark as he eased up beside Two-foot's trike.

"I'm your huckleberry…Big M's your dingleberry." he said and grinned, then sobered, "What's up?"

"Bro. Me and M are gonna see if we can find Kirk. Get us some retribution."

Skidmark's shoulders slumped and he shook his head.

"Damn! You guys just can't stay out of trouble, can you? I'd better tag along and take care of you."

The three of them sat until everybody else had left, then they pulled out with Two-foot in the lead.

They had traveled about a mile from the bar when they approached a dirt road leading off to the right. Two-foot pulled over on the shoulder. The other bikers pulled up beside him.

"I know he went in this direction, and I thought I saw a dust cloud. So I think he's down this way."

"You know anything about this road?" asked Big M.

"Yeah, I rode down it a couple of weeks ago. If I remember right it only goes about a mile then dead-ends at an old abandoned farmhouse. If he came this way, he's probably hiding out there."

"Well, you take the lead, and we'll stop when we're close enough to walk the rest of the way." said Skidmark.

"Yeah, and remember, he's got that dammed uzi!" added Big M.

Chapter Ten

Kirk pushed the shuttle bus down the dirt road as fast as he dared. It had gotten darker and it was hard for him to see. He had no idea where he was going, but knew he had to find a hiding place quickly. Noticing the giant dust-cloud behind him, he slowed his vehicle in hopes it wouldn't make so much dust.

He didn't want to turn on the lights for fear someone might see them and know where he was going.

"If I can hide out for a couple of hours," he thought to himself, "my boys should have converted all those misfit bikers by then, and I can go back and get my enlarged army on the move." He giggled again at the thought that in spite of some minor mishaps, he would soon be in control of the town, and his conquest of the world would be in action.

A short distance ahead he saw a hulking shadow that, when he got nearer, turned out to be an abandoned farmhouse. Slowing even further, he pulled off the road, bounced across the overgrown driveway and parked behind the house.

He sat in the silent bus still thinking about being King of The World. He giggled and fondled himself. He briefly thought about masturbating again, but decided to wait until he had his army on the march.

He stepped out of the vehicle and unzipped his pants and urinated against the wall of the house. He started wondering just how long it would take his army to take over the world. If everyone they fought, and bit, became one of them, surely it wouldn't take more than a few weeks.

Billy Kirk was picturing himself sitting on a jeweled throne in a magnificent palace with the world's most beautiful women waiting on him hand and foot. He recalled the woman back at the day care center and how good she had felt. His organ began to harden.

"Damn!" he whispered, "She sure had a nice ass." He began to slowly stroke himself. He was really starting to enjoy his hand when he thought he heard something in the darkness.

He paused, still holding himself, and tried to listen. He could hear the crickets chirping, and not too far away he thought he heard an owl, but didn't know for sure what it was. As he waited, listening, he began to go soft.

He sighed in disappointment. "Guess I'll wait." He muttered. Again he paused, trying to distinguish the different night sounds. The stars above were clear and bright, as was the moon, but nighttime in the country can be very dark and he wasn't used to it.

He sighed again and turned to get back into the bus.

"Hold it right there Asshole!" a voice demanded out of the darkness, and Billy Kirk nearly crapped in his pants.

"Whaa…" he managed to get out. Then another voice from behind him ordered.

"Stand still. If you move I'll blow your brains out!"

And before he knew what was happening, two men, then a third and ran up and grabbed him, throwing him against the wall. It took just seconds before they had his hands tied behind his back and had him sitting in the ground in front of the bus. One of them turned on the vehicle's parking lights.

"What are we going to do with him?" Big M asked.

"We can cut his throat and let him bleed out. said Skidmark, "It'd serve him right for raping that woman. And especially for what he did to Jynx!"

"Listen men, listen to me a minute," Kirk interrupted, "Let me go and join me and I'll share my power with you."

"Power, what power?" demanded Two-foot.

"My army can take over the whole world in a matter of weeks." Kirk continued eagerly, "and I'm going to be King. If you join me I'll give you high positions in my government. You'll have everything you ever wanted." His voice had grown more excited as he tried to convince the men.

"My boys are back at that biker bar and by now should have taken over. Those stupid bikers are probably part of my army right now. We just need to go back and give them some orders."

Two-foot looked at Big M and Skidmark.

"This fool sure is from the twilight zone or someplace, aint' he?"

"No shit! said Skidmark. He stepped into the light, bent over and backhanded Kirk across the face. The blow knocked Kirk over on his side. "We're those stupid bikers, you dumb mother-lover! Your boys didn't have a chance."

Kirk sat back up and looked at him, then the other two men.

"You…you can't be. My army can't be killed." He stammered.

"Yeah, well, guess again asshole." Grinned Big M. He pulled out a sword and showed Kirk the blade.

"They just kinda lost their heads when we brought out these." he said with a grin.

"Got an idea, guys," Two-foot said. He motioned them to follow him and they walked far enough away to be out of Kirk's hearing.

"The sheriff said it would be best, especially for us, if we weren't involved in this madness, right?"

Both his biker brothers nodded agreement.

"Let's duck-tape that bastard to a tree and leave him there. We'll call Dandy and have him tell the sheriff where he is. He'll be busted, and we'll still be in the clear."

Skidmark and Big M looked at each other for a moment, then back at Two-foot.

"Personally, I wouldn't mind cutting his throat." said Big M, "But what you said makes sense. But I've just gotta hit him at least once." He squatted down and faced Kirk.

"This one is for Jynx, you dick-breathed bastard!" he growled and slammed his right fist into Kirk's jaw. There was a loud crack as they heard the jaw- bone break and Kirk fell over on his side.

"Got any duck-tape in your pocket?" Skidmark asked his vertically challenged Brother with a smirk.

"No, but I sure do back in my tour pack." responded Two-foot. "You two stay here and keep an eye on the asshole, I'll go get the trike, That way I can haul your sorry asses back to your bikes when we're through."

"What the hell you standin' there for?" asked Big M, "get movin'"

"Wait a minute, I gotta take a leak." He stepped over the groaning Kirk, unzipped his fly and commenced to piss in the fallen man's face.

"Now that you mention it, I do too." said Skidmark. He joined Two-foot and Big M as they all three emptied their bladders in Billy Kirk's face.

In the days that followed, Two-foot eagerly read the newspapers for word about the incident at Little Critter. He had found one article about the original escape from jail and the murder of the two jail guards, and one convict. After that there was nothing.

It was exactly a week after the unbelievable fight with the zombies. And the day after the Biker Funeral for their fallen Brother Jynx, Two-foot's curiosity got the better of him and he and Partner took a ride out to Little Critter and Bugmees.

There were a couple of bikes there that he didn't recognize as he and Partner went inside.

"Hey Dandy!" he called out, "What's happenin' Bro?" He and Partner sat at a table and Sandy brought them each a beer. "Fix us up a couple of them thick burgers too, okay?" Two-foot ordered.

Dandy sat down at the table with them. He stared at Sandy's butt as she sashayed away.

"Ya know," he said, "my love for her is like diarrhea."

Partner burst out laughing. "Diarrhea!?"

"That's right," continued Dandy, "I just can't hold it in."

She reached over and patted his arm. "Well Dear, in matters of the heart, just follow your dick That's what you men usually do anyway."

She and Two-foot chuckled as Dandy grinned sheepishly. Then he grew serious. His voice grew soft as he spoke.

I sure am sorry about Jynx, man. It's a terrible thing to kill a man."

Two-foot shook his head sadly.

"I know Bro. But sometimes not killing is even worse." He lowered his voice even more too.

"You had to do it. Otherwise he mighta bit even more of us. You did good Dandy, no one faults ya on that deed." He looked around the bar, then continued.

"Speakin' of which, I haven't seen or heard anything about the fight." He said, "What's going on?"

Dandy glanced around to make sure no one could hear him then leaned closer.

"You wouldn't believe it, brother, but the F.B.I. and the CIA and just about every other government alphabet is involved in this thing." he whispered.

"What the hell for?" demanded Two-foot.

Partner leaned forward too, "You mean that crap really happened? They were zombies?"

She looked over at Two-foot, then gently laid her hand on his arm.

"I'm sorry for doubting you, honey," she said apologetically, "but, zombies!?"

He just chuckled, and smiled at her, "I was there, I was involved, and honey; I still don't believe it!" He turned back to Dandy.

"What else?"

Before Dandy could reply, the two men who had been sitting at the bar approached them.

"That your trike out there?" one of them asked.
"Yeah, good guess on your part." Two-foot answered in a not-too friendly manner.

"Nice. We were just wondering; do you ride much around here?"

"Now and then." The short biker responded.

"Know anything about all the excitement here last week?" the second man asked.

"Excitement?" said Two-foot with a puzzled look on his face, "I heard about all those guys breaking out of jail. And to tell you the truth, I hope they get away." He took a drink of his beer.

The two strangers looked at him and Partner for a moment, then one of them smiled in a friendly fashion.

"Oh, I'm sure the law will catch up to them sooner or later."

"Nice talking to you." The other man said, then they both walked out and the sound of their bikes starting up could be heard inside.

"Clever answer." Dandy told Two-foot, "Those guys have been hanging around for the past few days. I think they're Military Intelligence."

"Military Intelligence?" grinned Partner, "That's an oxymoron, isn't it?"

Dandy leaned forward again.

"Yeah, MI came in while the other government people were here, and they just took over everything. It seems that they had been investigating the dumping of several prostitute bodies down in the Hollywood area. Something about some kind of strange chemicals in their bodies. And some gang-bangers got part of the tag number of the car dumping one of them off. Guess who it was?"

"Kirk? No shit?"

"Yep; there's been a quiet man-hunt for him for several months."

"Well, they got him now." Two-foot said, "You did tell Taylor where we left him, didn't you?"

"Of course," Dandy nodded, "Told him I got an anonymous tip. But it won't do them any good to have him. He was totally insane when the cops got to him. He couldn't talk because his jaw got broken somehow. But he kept trying to growl about how he was the King of the World, or some stupid shit like that."

"Cops go out and search his place?" asked Two-foot.

"Dammed right they did. Found another body, and the jail transport bus. And I heard a rumor they found all of Kirk's papers with his chemical experiments written on them. Barney was there, and they swore him to secrecy, threatened to arrest him if he mentioned anything to anyone."

"Found another body, eh?" Said Two-foot more as a statement than a question. "I've been wonderin' what happened to that nineteenth zombie."

The three sat silently for a moment, each of them with their own private thoughts. Then Two-foot exclaimed bitterly;

"Shit! If the military got all his papers they'll be trying to make their own zombies pretty soon!"

"Yeah, man." Said Dandy with a serious look; "Scares shit out of me." Then he shrugged, "But hey; what the hell ya gonna do?" He and Two-foot looked each other in the eyes briefly, then Two-foot shrugged too.

"Hell, I'm goin' for a ride." He said as he rose from his seat with a final drink of his beer.

Partner stood and took his hand, "Sounds good to me Babe."

"Be careful." Dandy cautioned as they walked out, "no tellin' what you might run into down the road."

-30-

www.ingramcontent.com/pod-product-compliance
Ingram Content Group UK Ltd.
Pitfield, Milton Keynes, MK11 3LW, UK
UKHW020222250726
13967UKWH00001B/132

9 781105 277412